NOT MY ROMEO

KYLIE GILMORE

Cover design by Sweet 'N Spicy Designs

Published by: Extra Fancy Books

ISBN-13: 978-1-942238-0-96

Love at first fight!

1

Vince Marino was hours away from closing the twelve-million-dollar Clover Park Library project on behalf of Marino and Sons Construction, and he didn't need his dad second-guessing him.

"Dad, what're you doing here?" Vince pinched the bridge of his nose, working hard for patience. His dad had finished chemo four days ago and was supposed to be at home resting, not at work checking up on his son. His dad's deep brown eyes had bags under them. He looked wiped out, and Vince was more than ready to take over the reins at Marino and Sons, as he'd been promised from the beginning. Out of his five brothers, two biological, three step, Vince was the only one who'd stepped up to work in the family business. His dad had made him start at the bottom at eighteen on crew and work his way up. At thirty-four, sixteen long years later, Vince was still proving himself.

His dad grunted. "I just want to go over a few things before your presentation."

"I got it," Vince said, rolling up the construction plans for the project. They had computer renderings as well, but he liked to show the client on paper.

"You know how much we need this," his dad said. "And it's not in the bag until I sign on the dotted line."

Vince jammed his hands on his hips. "If you'd made me partner already, I could sign on the dotted line tonight."

"Tomorrow's soon enough." His dad ran a hand through his thinning brown and gray hair and sank heavily onto a chair. Vince was the spitting image of his dad from his large six-foot-three frame to the dark brown hair (no gray streaks for Vince yet), dark brown eyes, and strong nose and jaw. Watching his dad change as he got older was like glimpsing Vince's future self. Of course, his dad had looked a lot better before the chemo. He wasn't his usual vibrant, cheerful self either.

"Show me the budget again," his dad said with a wave of his hand. "I want to see the cash flow."

Vince bit back a curse only out of respect for his dad's condition. He flipped open the laptop and pulled the info up.

"So they're a definite on the municipal bond?" his dad asked.

"Yes. It passed the vote."

His dad squinted at the screen. "Remind me how much." He needed reading glasses, but refused to wear them.

"If private donations hit ten million, the bond will kick in for two million more."

"Who's running the private donation campaign?" his dad asked.

"The Friends of the Library committee," Vince said patiently. They'd been over this before.

"You think they'll hit their target?"

"They've already got half of it," Vince said. "This town is well connected. Gabe's been a big help with corporate sponsors."

At the mention of Vince's older stepbrother, his dad broke out in a wide smile. "Those city lawyer connections keep paying dividends. Good, good."

Vince pushed back the old jealousy that was his knee-jerk reaction when it came to Gabe. Until recently, he and Gabe had been rivals. Vince's fault, he knew. They'd been forced together as kids when Gabe's mom married Vince's dad. Vince had been twelve, Gabe fourteen, both of them the oldest in their respective families, both used to bossing their little brothers around, and they'd been forced to share a room. What was hardest for Vince was sharing his dad. He'd lost his mom when he was nine and had been tight with his dad. His dad had taken in his three new stepsons like they were his own. Looking back, he gave his dad a lot of credit for that, especially since his stepbrothers' biological dad was a complete asshole, but at twelve, and for longer than he'd like to admit, Vince had been nothing but pissed off.

Vince packed up the laptop and stood. "I'll call you tomorrow with the good news."

His dad stood and straightened Vince's tie for him. Anyone else and Vince would've slapped his hands away, but it was his dad. He accepted the annoyance and reached again for rapidly vanishing patience.

"You want me to come with?" his dad asked. "Just to listen and chime in if there's any questions."

Vince gritted his teeth. "I thought I was running it."

"You are. With supervision."

Vince met his dad's eyes with a hard stare. "Either you trust me or you don't. Which is it? Why have a Marino and Sons if you're never going to hand over the reins to your son? Because I don't see any other son lining up here for the job."

His dad jerked his chin. "Win the library project and we'll talk. You have to show me you can bring in business."

"I told you I got this!" Vince barked.

His dad squared his shoulders, still an impressive figure even after everything he'd been through. They were eye to eye. "I'll believe that when I see you at the groundbreaking ceremony."

And wasn't that just it in a nutshell? Gotta see it to believe it. Can't just believe in your firstborn.

"Thanks for your vote of confidence," Vince said before grabbing his stuff and heading for the door.

"Watch that mouth, son," his dad said.

Vince didn't reply. There was no respectful way to vent his anger. Instead he stepped outside, took in a deep breath of warm September air, got into his '69 Chevy Camaro and peeled out of the lot.

Sophia Capello strode through the Clover Park Library, head held high as if her father hadn't taken a million dollars from the company's coffers. And sank it into an alpaca farm.

As if her mother hadn't run off with the pool boy.

As if her younger brother hadn't just dropped out of college to follow his favorite punk rock band across the country.

And, most importantly, as if her family's business, Capello Construction, wasn't on the brink of collapse.

She stopped at the door of the meeting room and took a deep breath. A long oak table surrounded by black plastic chairs dominated the small room. And in those chairs sat nearly all middle-aged men—she assumed the town council and mayor—talking quietly amongst themselves. At the head of the table stood a whiteboard easel, which was where she'd be presenting Capello Construction's bid for the new library.

Her father, the head of Capello Construction, was currently holed up in his brother's apartment, nursing a broken heart (over her mother) with scotch and cheese puffs. He'd begged her to pull together this presentation at the last minute. The high price tag on the project was literally their last hope before bankruptcy.

She stepped inside and pasted on a smile. "Good evening, everyone. Thank you for allowing me to bid tonight."

She got right down to business, pulling some architectural drawings from her portfolio binder and leaning them against the whiteboard easel. Nerves skittered through her. She was not well-versed in construction, though she knew some things as an expert on historic architecture. Her dad had coached her, or more like she'd pried answers out of him while he'd stuffed his face watching *Scarface* on repeat. Her proposal depended on preserving the oldest part of the library while adding to it in a way that blended. She took a seat at the table and felt an intense stare directed right at her.

She looked up and nearly gasped at the male beauty glaring across the table at her. He was breathtaking—thick dark brown hair, deep chocolate brown eyes, chiseled cheekbones, a strong jaw, full sensuous lips. He was also large with a thick neck and massive shoulders that filled out his suit jacket, reminding her, for lack of a better word, of a lumberjack, except with nicer clothes. Her heart kicked up, but she held his gaze. It must be Vince, the hothead from Marino and Sons Construction. She'd never met him, but she'd heard about him over the years as her dad went off on his usual tirade against Marino and Sons Construction. The hostility and rivalry between her father and Vince's father had begun over a woman and escalated over the years to nothing short of all-out war. They were always bidding on the same projects, always undercutting each other's bids in bold moves to win the business, but, in the end, hurting only themselves by coming in at a lower price. She really didn't understand it. She suspected her dad's temper had a lot to do with it, which was why she had no worries about Vince's temper. Sophia was her father's daughter, with a lot more control.

"Who the hell is she?" Vince barked, making her hackles rise. "And why am I seeing construction plans?"

"Now, Vince," a man said.

Sophia glanced down at the neatly labeled paper name card perched in a binder clip in front of the man—Mayor Riggs. Figured. He was at the head of the table.

She spoke directly to Vince. "I'm Sophia Capello from Capello Construction. A last-minute addition to the agenda."

Vince's head snapped up, and she held his fiery gaze.

She went on. "I have a proposal for the library that includes looking at the historical significance of the building. Something I'm sure everyone in Clover Park would want to preserve."

Vince's jaw clenched. She looked back at him calmly.

Vince looked up and down the table. "Gentlemen, I've been jumping through hoops for months of meetings and presentations for the construction of this building by Marino and Sons. I thought this was a done deal. Why is this open for discussion?"

"We haven't signed any contracts yet," Mayor Riggs replied. "We'd like to hear from Ms. Capello tonight."

"Thank you, Mayor Riggs," Sophia said smoothly.

A muscle ticked in Vince's jaw. Sophia raised a brow, earning a dark scowl from Vince. Her pulse thrummed pleasantly. A little adrenaline before an important meeting could only help.

She smiled. "Shall we get started?"

2

_____

Vince sat there in his uncomfortable suit, seething as Sophia proceeded to charm the pants off the middle-aged horny men in the room, who couldn't take their eyes off her snug bright pink pants suit. It didn't help that the blazer was open and a skimpy black tank played peek-a-boo with ample cleavage as she moved. He tugged on his tie, pulling it away from his neck. Her long legs were in heels that screamed sex, with a thick strap around her ankles. Her toenails were pink. He tore his gaze from her toes back to her face as she smiled and pointed out all the features of the proposed construction for the library that was supposed to be his first project as full partner at Marino and Sons Construction. He'd been groomed for this position since birth and damned if Sophia Capello of all people was going to take that from him. His dad would keel over if he heard that Vince lost to his longtime competitor and personal nemesis Joe Capello. Or his representative.

Sophia was yammering on about the ancient part of the library. Like the original chandelier that had been found in the attic of the town hall, the circular iron stairway, the skylight, and the mosaic floor that would make a welcoming foyer and a statement about Clover Park and its long storied history. Yawn. Clover Park was nothing more than a small Connecticut town that had once been the country escape of the New York City wealthy elite and was now just a sleepy suburb. His idea for a modern sleek glass building was both a challenge to construct and offered views to the park across the street that was the highlight of its location. Who cared about the original brick front, which was, by the way, crumbling, or the marble columns by the front door that were more fitting to a larger Greek-style building, not a dinky brick library in disrepair on account of being built in fucking 1896. The addition to the library, built in the 1960s, was extremely outdated and too small for continued use.

Vince stifled a yawn as Sophia went on and on about the original fireplace—major fire hazard in a room full of books—and finally quieted. He stood immediately to take over the meeting, crossing to where she stood at the head of the table.

"Gentlemen," he began. "As we've discussed—"

"Excuse me," Sophia said with a smile to the seated men. "I wasn't quite finished yet."

He crossed his arms. "Finish."

She smiled sweetly at him, but her glittering dark brown eyes were full of challenge. His eyes locked with hers, ready to do battle. She gave him a small smile that was more of a *fuck you* than a smile and turned to the room. "Rather than go with a stark modern building, I'm proposing more brick blended to match the color of the original, starting with a single story and then moving up to two stories where the majority of the collection will be held." She flipped to the next drawing, which looked like a helluva lot of brick. Not cheap and definitely not capturing the view. "The slope of the property makes the two-story new construction a viable alternative."

He clenched his teeth. His was also a two-story construction, but with the demolition of the old structure.

She finally wound down. "Thank you for your time, gentlemen. I hope I've convinced you of the importance of preserving the historic architecture in a way that's still modern and functional. This town has such a proud history and it's up to us to preserve it for our children." She looked to some of the older men. "And our grandchildren."

Vince restrained himself from rolling his eyes. She didn't even live in town as far as he knew. Unfortunately, the men were eating it up.

"That's good," Mayor Riggs said, nodding enthusiastically.

"I liked it," someone else said. Lots of head bobbing and murmuring around the table.

"Gentlemen," Vince boomed, taking control of the meeting, "the primary feature of the library's location is its view of the park. That's why my design works best. We've got glass from floor to second-floor ceiling. A light, airy space centered in its natural environment, blending seamlessly. Brick cannot come close to this feel. And we've got environmental design built in, with passive solar in the back and construction standards at the highest energy efficiency." He paused. "You know my design, so let me just highlight the major features. One: natural beauty. Two: energy savings. Three: a less expensive budget than what's been proposed by Capello Construction. Thank you." His glare around the room challenged anyone to throw any of what he said into doubt. This was a no-brainer. They weren't building a freaking museum to the past. This was the time for new and modern.

Sophia shook her head. "While I'm sure we'd all like to save a few pennies, no one understands the importance of preserving Clover Park's illustrious history like I do. I'm an expert on historic architecture and work tirelessly to push historic designation through with the National Registry of Historic Places. Wouldn't it be nice to have a plaque on the front of the building declaring it a historic site?" She beamed a smile that had many of the men smiling back and nodding.

"And how long would that take?" Vince asked.

Sophia tossed her long wavy brown hair over one shoulder. "Applications take time, but I can help to make sure the forms go through efficiently."

"Uh-huh."

Sophia glared at him, her fiery nature doing something

weird to his insides, twisting them up and somehow heating him at the same time. Fuck. He was just as bad as these old geezers lusting after the beautiful woman. She was trying to take what was rightfully his, and he would not stand for that.

He addressed the mayor directly. "Marino and Sons is prepared to break ground as soon as next week. Our schedule is cleared for this project, which we thought, based on the number of meetings and approvals we've cleared already, was a mere formality. If you want your new library open by spring and on budget, then let's get started."

Mayor Riggs' mouth formed a flat line, and he slowly nodded. "Now, Vince, you make a good point there, and we all really liked your proposal." The other men hurried to agree. Brown-noser wimps. "But I think I speak for all of us when I say we also really liked Sophia's idea. There is something to be said for the history of Clover Park. We were one of the first towns in Connecticut to have a library."

"A historic designation could attract tourists," Sophia said. "And shoppers, since it's right on Main Street."

"I don't think tourists rush to visit plaques," Vince said.

Sophia frowned, causing a deep V to form in her forehead. "With my design, the new library will become a community hub." She pointed to the features of her plan. "A café, computer stations, and a small gallery to support local artists will attract even more visitors."

"We already have a café in town," Vince barked. Obviously she didn't do her homework. Damn interloper.

Mayor Riggs tapped his finger against his chin. Vince felt like bolting across the table and hauling him up by the shirt. *Make a decision, man. Have the balls to stand by your original word.*

One of the town councilmen whispered in the mayor's ear, and the mayor nodded. "We're going to look over both your plans, think it over, and give you our final decision next week." Mayor Riggs reached across the table to shake Vince's hand. "We appreciate your flexibility in this matter."

Vince shook his hand firmly. "See you next Tuesday," he

said in as well controlled a voice as he could manage given that he wanted to crack skulls.

Sophia stood and shook the mayor's hand. "I'll leave you with my designs. Thank you for your time." She strode out of the room, leaving the men with lingering gazes after her curvy ass.

Vince stood, jaw clenched tight over the howl he wanted to let loose. This had been in the bag. It was his. His first construction project with him in the lead. Fucking Capello Construction. They always undercut Marino and Sons' projects, but this was even worse, Capello hadn't even underbid them, yet they'd managed to get a foot in the door. One high-heeled, sexy supermodel foot. He'd never met Sophia before, and now he knew why. Capello was saving her as his secret weapon.

Vince grabbed his stuff and left, catching Sophia just as she left the building. "Yo, Sophia! Wait up!"

She kept going, forcing him to pick up the pace. He caught up to her on the sidewalk outside.

"Yo, Vince," she said, hand on her hip, all flip, like a twelve-million-dollar project didn't hang in the balance.

He sucked in air. "If you think for one minute I'm giving up and letting you—"

"See you at the next meeting!" She wiggled her fingers and left, hips swaying, long legs striding in those heels. His body reacted with an immediate boner that pissed him off, so he turned on his heel in the opposite direction. He circled around the block, hoping like hell she wouldn't still be in the parking lot when he got there because he couldn't be held responsible for his temper under these outrageous circumstances.

No sign of her. He felt let down somehow. His blood was boiling, he'd been itching for a fight, and she seemed more than capable of handling one. Hell, it probably would've been fun to go a couple rounds with her. Now what did that say about him? He had a screw loose. That's what.

∼

Vince headed to his older brother Gabe's place, still fuming. Gabe was a lawyer, and Vince wanted to sue. Breach of contract or something. It was a little after nine, so he figured he'd be up. He pulled up to Gabe's place, which used to be their parents' house. Vince had lived there from twelve on with his five brothers. He used to think of them as two real brothers (Nico and Angel) and three stepbrothers (Gabe, Luke, and Jared), but lately he just thought of them all as real brothers. He was getting soft in his old age, ever since Gabe and Zoe asked him to be godfather to their son. It meant something to Vince that they chose him as family when they damn well didn't have to.

He knocked on the front door and waited impatiently. The door swung open a few moments later.

"Hi, Vince," his sister-in-law Zoe greeted him with her sunny smile, bright brown eyes, and brown hair in a braid over one shoulder. She was cute as a button and had to reach up on tiptoe to give him a hug. He returned it, careful not to press into her pregnant belly. She stood back to let him in. "Come on in. What's up?"

He stared at her stomach, bulging in her giant maternity T-shirt nightgown. It had a cartoon picture of a baby where it would be curled up inside. "How's my boy?" he asked.

"He's kicking a lot." She took his hand and pressed it against her stomach. Something moved under her skin, shifting around. He suppressed a shiver. That was just freaky.

"Feel it?" she asked with a smile.

He didn't want to make her feel bad. She was incubating his godson, even if he did seem like an alien creature about to burst through her skin. "Sure did."

Gabe appeared with their dog, Fred, a medium-sized silver and black furball, trotting along his side. His stepbrother was fair with short cropped light brown hair and dark blue eyes. Fred started barking, like he'd just noticed Vince was there.

"Settle," Gabe said, and Fred shut up. Gabe wasn't a big guy, five nine or so, medium build, but his brother could hold his own, and the dog respected that.

"Sorry to barge in on you guys." Vince shoved a hand in his hair and backed up. He hadn't expected Zoe to be in her nightgown. "I'll go."

"Don't be silly," Zoe said. "We were just watching TV. Come in, I can tell something's bothering you. I was heading up to bed soon." She kissed Gabe, who looked after her, lust in his eyes, as she headed upstairs.

Vince didn't even know how Gabe worked around that belly. She was six and a half months along. He kept track. The baby was due December fifth, and Vince had already cleared his calendar.

Gabe finally tore his gaze from his wife and looked at him. "Beer?"

"Sure."

He followed him to the kitchen and sat at the island. He watched Gabe get the beer, still feeling like an ass for barging in on their love nest.

Gabe popped the cap off two beers and handed one to Vince. "What's up?"

Vince took a long swallow. "What's new with the baby?" As godfather, he felt it important to keep up to date on all the latest.

One corner of Gabe's mouth lifted. "He's good. Growing like he should. Nice and active."

"Good, good." Vince took another long swallow and a vision of feminine toes peeking out of high heels popped into his head. "I need to sue someone."

"You do?"

"Capello Construction."

Gabe took a pull on his beer. "Ooh, boy. Dad's always going off about them. What'd they do that was illegal?"

"They're trying to steal the Clover Park Library project right out from under me, coming in with a last-minute bid."

"Didn't they have an open call for proposals?"

Vince scowled. "Bah. I know I don't have a case. I'm just pissed off." He pounded his fist on the counter. "This was supposed to be the last meeting. The final signing on the dotted line, and then *she* walks in."

"She?"

"Their secret weapon. Capello sends in his supermodel daughter to turn heads. They're thinking with their little heads, nodding and smiling. Next thing I know they want to think about it! Make a decision next week." Vince gestured wildly. "She's going on and on about a fucking fireplace!"

Gabe held up a hand. "Slow down. Capello has a supermodel daughter? That's perfect for supermodel Vince."

Vince pursed his lips. "Fuck you."

"Sorry. Couldn't resist." He smirked and drank his beer.

"I'm not a supermodel, and you damn well know it."

"But you could've been." Gabe smirked some more. "We all know that story."

"That was one time." He jabbed a finger in the air. "One time some random lady stopped me in the city to give me her card. You guys never let me live that down."

Not one of his brothers gave him respect.

Gabe chuckled and shook his head. "This is like the Montagues and the Capulets. Warring families. Two star-crossed lovers."

Vince set his beer down. "What are you yammering about?"

"Shakespeare," Gabe said. "*Romeo and Juliet*. The long family rivalry with the Montagues and the Capulets. You and Sophia, two star-crossed supermodel lovers of the rival Marinos and Capellos." He snorted.

"Shut up, brainiac. There's no lover situation here." He drank his beer and thought some more on the way he'd been blindsided tonight. "There was a verbal agreement between me and the mayor. That's got to mean something."

Gabe shook his head. "Not enough. Sorry."

"This is a twelve-million-dollar project," Vince boomed. "We need this one. Ever since Dad got sick, business has been down. This was supposed to be the one that put me in charge. Gave everyone confidence that Marino and Sons could do well under new leadership. Me." It was up to Vince to keep the business going. He'd fucking earned this. Sixteen years of hard work without a single complaint.

Gabe took a pull on his beer. "You got anything else in the pipeline?"

"Nothing much. Just maintenance jobs. A new roof for a strip mall. Nothing like this."

"Maybe you can work something out with her. If the decision goes her way, you can still have a piece of it as a subcontractor."

"I guess." Not that his dad would ever agree to that. The animosity whenever his dad heard the name Joe Capello was outrageous. It had started over a woman way back in high school. It was Vince's mother that both men loved. Obviously she chose Vince's father, but the hostility between the two men continued and escalated as they became vicious competitors in a tight construction market. Capello underbid as many of their projects as he could, which forced Marino and Sons to go even lower if they needed the business. And they really needed this library project. Vince knew better than anyone Marino and Sons would be in serious trouble if he didn't land a big project soon.

If he did work with Sophia, he'd want the lion's share of the job. A majority stake. He drained his beer and recycled the bottle in the pullout drawer by his brother.

"I'm not splitting the project fifty-fifty," Vince said.

"Of course you're not."

Vince gave Gabe a pat on the cheek that was a near slap. "Thanks, bro."

Gabe returned the near slap. "Go play nice with the supermodel, Romeo," the smartass said.

3

Vince ripped off his shirt and rifled through his closet for another one. This week had been shit. His dad was pissed that he didn't come back with a contract. Vince had told his dad the town council wanted another week to decide. He'd left out the part about Capello Construction's bid. He knew the minute the name Capello came up, his dad would be all over this project, and Vince didn't want that. This was his baby.

He'd finally decided to take Gabe's advice and try to work something out with Sophia ahead of time. He had a bad feeling those town council bozos were going to side with her idea just because of all that crappy history stuff. He yanked on a white button-down shirt he usually wore with his funeral suit. Suited his mood. Sophia had agreed to meet him tonight to talk. She'd picked some fancy-pants restaurant, Le Jardin, in uppity Greenport, where she lived. Why couldn't they just have gone for pizza near his house in Eastman?

He looked in the mirror, frowned, and added a tie. He felt like he was choking. He yanked off the tie and threw it across the room. He was already tired from the hard physical labor he'd put in today, along with his crew, ripping off old roof tile from a strip mall. He liked to kick back with a beer on Friday night, not put on a monkey suit and drive thirty minutes away to pretend he was as classy and sophisticated as Sophia. But he had to fake it, had to make her see that working with him was a good idea. If it came to that. Hell, he could feel the whole thing slipping through his fingers. They would've signed off with Marino and Sons then and there if they really wanted them. He paced back and forth, his back and shoulders tense as all hell. He rolled his neck. A shower would relax him. He still had twenty minutes.

He stripped down and headed for the bathroom. A few minutes later, he stood under the spray and mentally rehearsed what he'd say. He should probably hold off on the business talk until they'd eaten. Maybe get some wine in her. Women were always more agreeable after a glass of wine. Why did he have to deal with Sophia at all? What the hell had happened with her dad, the man who owned Capello Construction?

A short while later, he stepped out of the shower, dried off, and grabbed the first shirt with no wrinkles from the closet. Fuck the tie. And no blazer either. They could kick him out if it came to that. He didn't want to go to Le Jardin anyway.

Sophia hadn't been at all surprised to get a message from Vince at her Capello Construction voicemail. He'd been furious at their last-minute bid for the library business. What did surprise her was his tone, a deep, melodic voice offering a truce and an invitation to dinner. She accepted his invitation in a return message on his voicemail and suggested Le Jardin because the food was good and it was a short walk home if the meeting went horribly wrong. Which was entirely possible if he had a temper to match hers.

So here she was, sitting alone at Le Jardin, wearing her little black dress and beginning to feel stood up. Annoyed over how late he was, she finished her glass of sauvignon blanc and signaled the waiter for a second glass. *I have better ways to spend my Friday nights than sitting alone in a restaurant.*

She sighed and took some bread from the basket in front of her. She missed her old social life in Brooklyn. Her friends never wanted to visit her in Greenport. It was boring compared to the city. She'd moved in to her parents' house a month ago at her dad's request to housesit (he feared someone would rob them if it appeared empty) while he holed up at his brother's apartment, trying to avoid anyone he knew. She had a roommate in Brooklyn, so she knew her place was fine. Her mom was living it up in Florida with Manuel. Do *not* think about it.

She tapped her manicured nails on the table. Maybe she should just order something to go. When the waiter came back with her wine, she'd order the lemon rosemary chicken and head home. She ate some bread and casually looked around the restaurant, mostly couples, most of them sitting with nothing to say to each other. Geez, that was depressing. She never wanted to be like them. To be like her parents had been before the separation. Her dad still hoped to reconcile. Her mom had requested a divorce.

The wine arrived, and she forced a smile for the waiter. "I'm ready to order," she said.

"Very good," the man said. "Would you like to hear the specials?"

She glanced up to find Vince strutting toward her—a lumberjack with style. He wore a light blue button-down shirt open at the collar, revealing tanned skin from working outdoors. His hair was damp, like he'd just showered. He was such an imposing presence with that height and build that heads were turning as he approached. Definitely not her type. She liked cultured, refined men who appreciated history and architecture, her two loves.

He leaned down and kissed her cheek. "Sorry I'm late."

She jolted at the unexpected affection. She'd thought he'd come in ready to blast her. His woodsy, masculine scent only emphasized his lumberjack fresh-from-the-woods appeal. He must be trying to throw her off her game, acting the part of doting boyfriend. They barely knew each other.

They were enemies. Or at the very least, competitors.

He took the seat across from her and glanced at the waiter. "Bring a bottle of whatever she's drinking."

"Very good, sir." The waiter left.

"So, what's good here?" Vince asked with a smile.

She cocked a brow. "You're in a good mood."

"I'm having dinner with a beautiful woman. What's not good about that?"

She took a sip of wine, considering this surprising change in his attitude. "You can't sweet-talk me into handing over the library project, so you can drop the act."

He leaned forward and lowered his voice. "I could sweet-talk you into just about anything, darling, but that's not what this is." He leaned back. "This is just two people working out a deal. Once we finish eating. I want to enjoy my meal without any indigestion, *capisce*?"

She smirked at the Italian phrase, the subtle tip of his hat that they both had Italian heritages, that they were the same. Even though they both knew the long-standing hostility between their two fathers. She was sure his father must have a temper to match her father's for the feud to have continued for so many years, which meant Vince would've heard plenty about it. He was good, she'd give him that. "*Come sta la sua famiglia?*" She'd spent a year in Italy as an exchange student.

He broke out into a wide smile. "*Mi famiglia* is great, thanks. And yours?"

Her family was terrible. Tears unexpectedly stung her eyes, and she blinked rapidly, trying to cover. "Fine," she managed.

"How's your dad? I thought I'd be dealing with him."

"He's recovering from an illness." Lovesickness, she added silently.

He stared at her. "Nothing serious, I hope."

"No, he'll have a full recovery."

Vince nodded once and pulled out the menu.

The waiter arrived with the bottle of wine. He poured a small amount in a glass for her to sample. She nodded her acceptance, and he poured Vince a glass. She was still working on her second glass. They listened to the specials and placed their order.

Silence descended. Sophia was trying very hard not to think of the mess her family had left her, but it was hard not to. She was well used to fixing things for her family, but this time had been different. Her dad had made an unusually emotional desperate appeal for her to return to Greenport and take care of both the house and the business. She'd agreed, knowing she could still commute to the city for work, a forty-minute drive, and work from home sometimes. She'd unfortunately been taking a lot of time off from her real job, trying to keep the family business from going under. But her dad had been in a really dark place since her mom had left. And now here was Vince just waiting to make her life even more difficult. She set down her wine and took a deep breath.

"Maybe we should just get this over with," she said at the same time as he said, "I'm going to be a godfather."

And then he pulled out his cell phone and showed her an ultrasound picture of a tiny, beautiful baby. "It's a boy," he said, pointing out the requisite equipment.

"Oh, he's so perfect," she said. "So precious. Whose baby is it?"

"My older brother Gabe's," he said, looking at the picture and smiling. Her heart stuttered at the beauty of that moment —one gorgeous man adoring a baby. "He's due December fifth."

She swallowed over the lump in her throat. "Have they picked out a name?"

"Not yet. I keep suggesting Vince, but for some reason, they're not going for it." He flashed a smile, and she smiled back. Her gaze locked with his.

She stopped smiling.

He stopped smiling.

The tension was palpable, a very inconvenient frisson of electric attraction ran through her, and she panicked. "So!" she said brightly. "More wine?" She grabbed the bottle and went to pour him another glass, but he covered it with his hand.

"It's still full," he said solemnly.

She forced a cheery smile, avoiding his eyes. "More for me!" She topped off her own glass and took a sip, all too aware that he was staring at her.

"So what do you do when you're not bidding on library construction projects?" Vince asked.

"I work for a consulting firm. They send me out to look at historic buildings, evaluate them, and help them fill out the paperwork for tax credits and applying for the National Register of Historic Places. Things like that. It's fascinating, actually. What about you?"

"I build things," he said, deadpan.

She drained her glass of wine, knowing she was out of her element, but desperate to save her family's business. If she could just hold it together long enough for her idiot brother, Mike, to stop following that damn band, graduate, and take over Capello Construction as he was supposed to, everything would work out.

"Well, duh," she said. She poured herself a third glass of wine.

He cocked a brow. "How many glasses of wine have you had?"

"Just two."

He took her glass and set it next to his own. "You're done."

"What the hell! You're not my father." She reached for it, and he snagged her wrist.

"You can drink all you want after I leave, but I'd like to have a semi-coherent conversation with you about business before I go."

"Ooh, semi-coherent," she mocked. His grip on her wrist was warm, firm, and she liked it way too much. "Big talk."

He gave her a knowing look. "You're just looking for a fight, aren't you? You need someone strong to bump up against. Not one of those metrosexual types you usually date."

She lifted her chin, her heart pounding against her ribs.

She yanked her wrist out of his grip. "What do you know about who I date?"

"I guessed. Someone who can spend twenty minutes talking about a hundred-year-old fireplace needs someone nerdy to listen."

She huffed. "You're wrong."

"Am I?" He bit back a smile and sipped his wine, all smug-like.

She reached for her wine again, and he snagged her wrist halfway there. "I can do this all night," he said in a husky voice that made her stomach flutter.

She glanced toward the door. The hell with him. She'd go into that next town council meeting, charm the council members, and win that project.

Vince's grip on her wrist tightened. "Don't even think about bolting."

"Let go. You're hurting me."

He loosened his grip, but he didn't let go.

Her temper flared. "Is this how you treat all your dates?"

"You are not my date," he said. "You are business."

She swallowed and willed herself to calm the fuck down. She didn't need him. And she sure as hell didn't need all the aggravation that always seemed to land in her lap. "You can go to hell," she muttered.

"I'm taking you down with me, darling."

And damn if the words didn't make her throb. This was terrible. Horribly inconvenient. And he was still holding her wrist. His rough, calloused hand against the sensitive underside was doing strange things to her insides.

She glared at him. "Fuck this," she said just loud enough for him to hear. Her cheeks heated. She rarely cursed, but wine always seemed to loosen her tongue. Especially when she was pissed off.

His response was one slow, sexy, very knowing smile that made her squirm. "Business first, sweetheart, then pleasure." He laughed.

She yanked her wrist out of his grip, grabbed her purse, and left.

4

———

"Ah, hell," Vince muttered, setting his napkin and some bills on the table and following Sophia out the door. Women were so damn touchy. And this one. What a piece of work. She hurried down the sidewalk in stilettos, like she was wearing sneakers. He picked up the pace. "Where are you running off to?"

"Home," she hollered and kept going.

He caught up with her. "I'm coming with you."

Her dark brown eyes flashed, and she tossed her long dark brown hair over her shoulder. "Like fucking damn hell you are."

He chuckled. She strung curse words together like she didn't know how to use them. So damn cute. He fought back a grin and lost. "The mouth on you. Seriously, though. We need to talk."

She glared at him, fire burning in her eyes, and everything in him coiled and tightened with raw lust. Fuck, this was not what he needed right now. He needed to work out a deal with her and put Marino and Sons back on track.

"So talk," she bit out.

He knew, just knew, he wasn't going to get anywhere with her so furious with him. He rarely apologized, rarely softened, but just this one time for his dad's sake, he had to. For Marino and Sons, he told himself. Take one for the team.

"I'm—" *Cough*. He cleared his throat. It was harder to get out than he'd thought. "I'm—"

"What? An obnoxious arrogant fucking damn hell jerk who laughs inappropriately at women trying to do their fucking damn hell job?"

Vince forced a straight face. He didn't dare open his mouth. He might laugh again.

"Yeah, you are." She kept walking.

He kept up with her. "I'm sorry if I was inappropriately… I'm not supersensitive or whatever. Can we just talk about the project?"

She picked up the pace. The woman could really move in stilettos. He kept up.

"Go home, Vince."

No way in hell he was going home. She'd never agree to meet with him again, and he was not going into that next town council meeting without knowing he was at least getting a piece of the pie. He followed a step behind her for a couple of downtown blocks. She stopped at the traffic light before the bridge. Across the bridge were a row of homes along the riverbank, each of them large and expensive. Of course that's where she'd live.

"Which mansion is yours?" he asked.

She turned. "I swear I will pepper spray you if you don't leave me the fucking damn hell alone!"

He narrowed his eyes. "Would you just calm the fucking damn hell down?"

She glared at him. "You don't get to tell me what to do." She turned and stepped out into the road.

"Watch out!" He saw it like slow motion, a Ferrari speeding around the turn, Sophia about to get clipped. He grabbed her, yanking her back, and crashed to the sidewalk with her in his arms. His head hit concrete, a flash of light went off behind his eyes, and then everything went black.

~

Sophia's heart was racing. Vince had saved her. That red car. It was coming so fast, she'd barely had time to react before he'd grabbed her. And now the man underneath her was eerily still.

She got off him and knelt down next to his head. "Vince! Are you okay? Oh no, oh no." She listened closely near his mouth. He was breathing. She pulled her cell out, about to call nine-one-one, when he groaned. "Vince! Talk to me! How bad is it? How many fingers am I holding up?" She held up three fingers in his face.

"Three." Her hero slowly got up, holding the back of his head. "Damn, that's gonna be a goose egg."

"Let me see." She peered at the back of his head. There was some blood. "Come on. I'm a block away. I'm getting you ice and a doctor."

"No doctor."

Sophia knew better than to argue. She'd convince him after she got him settled at home. "Can you walk okay?"

He took a step and limped. Oh God, this was all her fault. If her temper hadn't gotten the better of her, she never would've run off, she never would've almost gotten run over, and he never would've had to save her. She scooted up against his side and put his arm around her shoulders. "You can lean on me," she said.

He did, and he was heavy. Six foot something of solid man was tough for a woman in stilettos, but she bore up under the weight because it was the least she could do. She was five foot ten, so at least he didn't have to lean down too far. They slowly made their way to the house. She got him inside and directed him to the living room sofa. He slumped heavily onto it.

She slapped his face rapidly. "Don't fall asleep. You might have a concussion."

He snagged her slapping hand. "Ice," he bit out.

She hurried to get it and grabbed some Tylenol and a glass of water too. She handed him the ice pack and set the other things on the end table next to him. She wrung her hands together. "How do you feel?"

"I feel—" he winced as he put the ice pack on the back of his head "—like I just took a header to the sidewalk."

She wrung her hands some more. "What can I do? How many fingers am I holding up?" She held up four.

"Four. You know what would make me feel better?"

She leaned forward. "What?"

"A little thank you."

"Thank you!" she gushed. "I would've said that earlier, but I was so worried. Thank you for saving me. I'm sorry I ran off like that. Sometimes my temper—"

He held up a hand. "Got it." He shook out some pills and swallowed them down. "You got anything to eat? I'm a little light-headed from not eating lunch, and we didn't get to dinner."

He was hungry. He couldn't be that bad off if he had an appetite. She blew out a breath of relief. "Yes, of course. I'll make us some sandwiches. Be right back."

He closed his eyes. Maybe light-headed was bad, though. Maybe he had a concussion or some serious head trauma. She slowly backed out of the room, watching him in case he suddenly slumped over.

"I'm fine," he said. How did he know?

She darted into the kitchen. She quickly put together two turkey sandwiches on whole wheat bread and returned to find him in the same position, eyes closed. "Vince?"

He slowly opened his eyes.

"Are you okay?"

"I've been better."

She sat next to him and handed him the sandwich. He took a big bite. "Thanks," he said around the sandwich.

She took a bite of her sandwich. Then she remembered his ankle and hurried to get the ottoman. "Here, you can put your feet up. I'll get you more ice for the ankle."

He put his feet up. She rushed from the room and returned with another ice pack. She quickly lifted his pant leg and draped the ice pack over his ankle. Her pulse thrummed through her. His calf was muscular, some dark hair, not overly much, tanned. Very manly. And beautiful.

"Thank you, Sophia."

Her insides fluttered. The way he said her name. His voice sounded like it could be on the radio—melodic, deep, reverberating through her mind. She tore her gaze from his calf to meet his eyes, which were softer now. Probably because he was in so much pain.

Guilt stabbed at her, and she sat next to him again. "I'll take you to the emergency room as soon as you're done eating."

"I'm done, and, no, you won't."

She glanced over, shocked that he'd finished the sandwich so quickly. "Are you sure? Are your eyes dilated?" She peered into them. It was hard to tell, they were such a deep brown surrounded by dark lashes. She held up two fingers in his face.

He grabbed her fingers and held them. "Please stop making me count."

"I heard that's how you check for concussion."

He released her fingers. "I'm fine. I've taken worse headers playing football."

She peered worriedly into his face. He was hard to read, sort of blank. Was he losing focus? Was that a symptom? "But you weren't wearing a helmet this time."

"Didn't wear a helmet wrestling my brothers either." He leaned back. "I've got five of them, and they liked to pile on me because I'm the biggest. That's where most of my scars come from."

She cringed. "Really?" That sounded terrible.

"Yeah."

"Are you sure you're okay?" She leaned closer, peering into his eyes again, trying to figure out if they were dilated. "Are you losing focus?"

He looked away. "I'm sure."

"Oh." She took his hand. It was rough, but so warm, she didn't want to let go. "I'm really sorry."

He squeezed her hand. "I'll live."

"Thanks again for saving me. I was being a jerk."

He slipped his hand from hers. "You're welcome. I was being a jerk too. Unprofessional."

They sat for a few moments in silence.

"Should we talk about the library?" she asked, picking up her sandwich.

"Could I take a rain check on that? My head's not great right now."

She turned to him. "I knew it. What can I do?"

"Just sit with me a bit. Give the Tylenol a chance to kick in; then I'll head out."

"I'll drive you home. You shouldn't be driving like this."

"All right. I'll have my brother come back with me for the car tomorrow."

She set her sandwich down, her appetite trumped by concern for the man she'd been nothing but rude to—she'd cursed him out like nobody's business—and he'd *saved* her. No one had ever put themselves out there like that on her behalf. Her throat felt tight. There was no reason to cry, she told herself. He was fine.

She shifted, leaning her head against his shoulder, trying to bring him comfort. He sat very stiff and still. The pain must be terrible. She raised her head and met his eyes. He gazed down at her with those deep chocolate brown eyes framed by long lashes. A surge of affection rushed through her, and she kissed him, a soft brush against his lips. A question, waiting for an answer.

The answer was no.

His lips were not kissing her back. At all. She pulled away, embarrassed.

He leaned forward and took the ice pack off his ankle. "I should go." He was looking around the room, looking at everything but her.

She quickly stood. "Of course." She grabbed her purse and led the way to the garage. He followed at a slow, limping pace behind her. She hurried back to him. "Lean on me."

"I got it."

She didn't know which made her feel worse, his obvious

pain or his rejection. She felt like an idiot confusing a rescue for any feeling on his part. She was so used to doing the rescuing that she didn't know how to respond. A simple thank you was all that he'd asked. Cheeks burning with mortification, she headed for her car.

5

———

Vince followed Sophia to the garage with only one thought in mind—he had to get out of there fast. As strange as it sounded, he'd never had a woman kiss him. He was always the aggressor. He took what he wanted when he wanted, and that was that. Her mouth had been soft and yielding. And she smelled like roses with a hint of spice, sexy and sweet. It took everything he had not to kiss her back.

Sophia was a complication that he damn well didn't need.

He stopped short when he saw her car—a Mini Cooper. "I'm supposed to fit in that thing?"

"It's surprisingly roomy," she said, walking past him with her flowery sex scent.

He didn't move. She peered at him from across the roof of the car. "It's either this or I drive your car, but then I'd need a cab ride back. It could take a while for the cab to show up, and I have a feeling you want me out of your hair, so *get in.*"

With that, she got into the driver's seat, leaving him no choice but to follow suit. He bent his tall frame, wincing at the pressure on his ankle, he must've twisted it as he fell, and squeezed into the passenger seat. He adjusted the seat, pulling it back as far as it would go. There was just enough room for his long legs.

"See, you fit," she said, grabbing the stick shift and putting it in gear. His dirty mind immediately went to her grabbing his stick. He scrubbed a hand over his face.

"Your head hurting?" she asked after she'd pulled into the street.

"Yeah."

"I'll get you fixed up. Where am I heading?"

"Eastman." He rattled off the address in the town next to Clover Park. He owned his own home, a dilapidated place that used to be the carriage house for a large Victorian on an estate. He'd bought it because it was cheap, and he knew he could fix it up in his spare time. It was a work in progress.

He cracked the window open, finding her rose scent too damn distracting in the confines of the car. All he could think about was burrowing into her neck, her cleavage, every damn place, and breathing her in.

"Would the radio make your headache worse or better?" she asked.

"Depends on the music."

She turned it to a classic rock station. "Okay?"

"Yeah." This was the same station he listened to. He closed his eyes, not liking how he was finding things they had in common when he was supposed to be taking control of this situation and staking his claim on the project. He let out a long breath, exhausted from his day.

He startled awake a moment later when she shouted, "Don't fall asleep!"

He straightened. "What's wrong with you? I'm tired."

"I'm getting you checked out. You could have a concussion. Eastman has a hospital, right?"

"I told you I'm fine."

"Men don't know when to ask for help. We're going."

He clenched his jaw, beyond annoyed. "My brother is a doctor. I'll call him and tell him what happened. If he says I have to go, I'll go."

"Call him right now."

He pulled out his cell and hit Jared's number. Voicemail.

Dammit. He was probably doing another long shift at the hospital. He was an orthopedic surgeon. He glanced at Sophia, who gripped the steering wheel with both hands, worry etched into her face. He faked it to put her mind at ease and get himself off the hook.

"Hey, Jared, it's Vince. Listen, I took a header to the sidewalk. Got a goose egg on the back of my head." He paused. "Yeah, upper back of the head. Uh-huh." He nodded at Sophia with a look that he hoped said *look how helpful my doctor brother is.* "No dizziness, no double vision. Just a headache. You think it's a concussion, or can I just sleep it off?" He paused. "Great. Thanks, buddy." He hung up and turned to Sophia. "He says I should be fine."

"Nice try," Sophia said. "I heard that voicemail beep when you first called."

He muttered a curse under his breath.

"It's the least I can do after you saved me," she said. Somehow the words felt like payback. And not for saving her. For that kiss and not returning it.

"You always get what you want?" he asked.

"Yes, Vince, I always get what I want," she said in a voice dripping with sarcasm. "That's why I'm trying to save Capello Construction single-handedly with nothing but a degree in historic architecture to back me up. This is exactly how I want to spend my life, taking care of the house and business for my screwed-up family."

A pang of unwanted sympathy struck his heart. He had no idea what the deal was with her family, but it was clear she was out of her element. He wasn't going to ask about her family, though, because he knew if he opened that can of worms, he'd likely find himself uncomfortably close to being on her side.

He was starting to like her.

This was a big problem.

"Lucky you," he said.

"I'm sorry," she said quietly. "That slipped out. You don't need to hear about my problems." She nodded once. "I'm fine. It's you we have to get fixed up."

Two hours later, he finally walked in the door of his place. Sophia had carried through on her threat to take him to the emergency room. The doctor said he was fine. He knew it and had given Sophia an immediate "I told you so" that had her rolling her eyes. She followed him into his house, insisting on making sure he got in okay.

She gasped when she stepped into the living room. "Vince! Was this a barn or a stable? I love the ceiling!" She walked around the living room with its high ceilings and post and beam construction.

"It was a carriage house." He should've known a history buff would get off on his place. "I restored the floors myself."

She looked down at the wide-planked original pine hardwood floors, squatting down to run her fingers over them. "Wow. When was this place built?"

"Eighteen ninety."

"O-o-oh," she breathed, rushing to the floor-to-ceiling fieldstone fireplace and running her hand over the stone. She turned to him, her expression open and eager. "Can I take a tour?"

He stifled a groan. It would be so easy. Take the tour…and here's my bedroom.

He could not have her. His dad would kill him if he got involved with Sophia. First, he'd disown him; then he'd kill him.

Besides, business was business. He needed her to leave. Like right now.

"Bye, Sophia. It's been…a night."

Her expression immediately closed. "Right. I'll see you at the meeting."

"Thanks for the ride." He limped toward the stairs, wanting nothing more than to crash in bed, but guilt over squashing her history-buff hopes nagged at him. "I'll call you for a rain check on tonight. We'll talk. You can take the tour."

"Okay."

He could hear the smile in her voice and didn't trust himself to look at her. His defenses were weak. He couldn't afford to be soft around her. At least one part of him had gotten that message. He kept going and heard the front door quietly close behind her. He collapsed into bed, his last thought of her soft lips pressing against his.

6

———

Sophia had really not expected to hear from Vince again. When he hadn't called the next day after their disastrous dinner meeting, she'd thought he'd blown her off and with good reason. She'd nearly gotten him killed, made him go to the emergency room, and kissed him against his will. Not to mention all her rude cursing. Some crack negotiator for this project she was turning out to be. But here she was, heading to his place on a Sunday for an afternoon meeting. He'd even offered to give her a tour of his house, which made her giddy with excitement. So what if she was a little nervous about seeing him after that embarrassing kiss? She'd just pretend it never happened.

He'd better not bring it up.

He seemed to enjoy teasing her. Whatever. She could give as good as she got.

Driving in the bright September sunshine, she caught a glimpse of the original Queen Anne-style main house down the street before pulling around the long driveway of the carriage house. Ooh, she breathed as she drove through a canopy of hundred-year-old maple trees lined up on both sides of the driveway, welcoming visitors with their fiery orange leaves blowing in the gentle breeze. She'd missed all this beauty when she'd last been here because it had been pitch black. She parked in front of the detached garage in back and turned toward the house. The light blue wood-shingled house was even more gorgeous in the light of day.

She approached the back stone patio with a portico, where Vince was already seated, wearing dark shades. An opened beer sat on a nearby table. He hadn't shaved and the five o'clock shadow was pronounced. He didn't smile either, just sat there looking cool, detached, and a little dangerous. And he was so large. He was the kind of man that would want to be in charge. Of everything.

Sophia was not in the habit of letting anyone walk all over her.

She fervently wished she'd worn a tank instead of this sweltering cotton long-sleeved tunic. The weather was unseasonably warm for September. She was *not* hot for Vince.

She made a big show of studying the house and not him. "You have a tower!" That was actually really cool. The front of the house looked like a big stable, and she hadn't noticed the tower peeking out the back on her drive in.

"Yeah, you can't go up there," he said. "I haven't made it to that part of the house yet. It's a never-ending fix-it project."

"Was it for hay?" Still looking at the tower, not the devastatingly handsome man with bulging muscles in a T-shirt and jeans.

"No. It has a couple of rooms for staff that lived here to take care of the horses and carriages. Beer?"

"No, thanks." She took a seat in a cushioned chaise lounge across from where he sat and risked a look at him. He took a long swallow of beer, and his Adam's apple moved up and down in that thick neck. Why was he so thick, like everywhere? His neck, his shoulders, chest, biceps, those massive thighs. She felt all petite and light, which was saying something for a five-foot-ten woman. He wouldn't have a soft touch, wouldn't be gentle. He'd be rough, firm, probably toss her around a bit.

He'd *manhandle* her.

She crossed her legs over the throbbing. She hadn't thought this through. Meeting at his house was a dumb idea.

She'd only been thinking of the history of his place. *Yes, think about history.* She took a deep breath, imagining when this had been some gentleman's estate, probably some rich guy from New York City who summered here. The backyard was small with a short crumbling stonewall delineating the property line.

"Tour first or business?" he asked.

She stood abruptly, the history fanatic in her beyond excited. "Tour."

"Figured." He stood and his jeans, worn and snug, made her stare in an unseemly way. What was wrong with her? She was positively ogling him, and she was not an ogler. He turned toward the door, and she stared some more at that tight ass. "Come on."

He had a slight limp, and she belatedly remembered to ask how he was doing. "Is your head okay? Your ankle looks like it still hurts."

"I'm fine," he said over his shoulder. So tough.

She followed him inside through glass French doors to a dining room with a long blue table and wood chairs painted in a variety of bright colors. The ceiling was post and beam, the floor a glossy wide-planked pine like the living room. Hanging pendulum lights lit the space over the table. Vince had style. The combination of modern and classic was stunning. She turned to him where he stood at the entrance to the room. He'd taken off the shades, and his expression was frustratingly hard to read. She pushed that thought aside. Who cared if he was thinking about that kiss? She was touring a beautiful historic carriage house and that was what she came here for, nothing else. "Did you do the interior design?"

He shrugged. "Just picked out the furniture, built a few pieces, and installed some lights."

"Did you build this table?" It was a simple Shaker style, very elegant.

"Yeah."

"It's beautiful."

He grunted in response. Not much for compliments, it seemed.

She headed to the far end of the room and peeked around a partial wall to find a small galley kitchen with a breakfast bar, sink, stovetop, and a few cabinets. "Cute kitchen," she said.

"You want a drink before we get started?" He indicated the refrigerator pressed against one side of the room.

She could tell he was anxious to finish the tour, but her curiosity drove her on. "No, thanks."

She headed to the next room, the large living room she'd seen the last time she was here. It was filled with light from oversized windows. "Did you add the windows?"

"Those two were added." He pointed, indicating the windows he'd added on the side. "The frames of the others are original. I switched out the glass to double-glazed for the insulation."

She rushed to the next room, a cozy space with built-in bookcases and an arched window. The bookcases were empty, except for one shelf with a collection of picture books by Allie Reynolds. "Is she your favorite author?"

He shoved his hands in his pockets, looking uncomfortable. "She's my stepmother."

"Oh." She took in the mostly empty space. "A piano would look nice in here."

"I don't play."

I do, she thought. What was she doing? Imagining herself here. Ridiculous.

"The rest is still in progress," he said. "Some areas have torn-up walls, exposed wiring. Not pretty."

She was dying to see upstairs, but she restrained herself. "Okay, let's get started."

He inclined his head and led the way down a narrow hallway back out to the open dining room and the back patio. Since his back was to her, she ogled his ass, along with his massive shoulders and broad back. He was awfully solid, lumberjack rugged. They didn't make men like this in her Brooklyn neighborhood, more like hipsters in black-rimmed glasses with goatees. Her type, in other words.

He flopped onto a long cushioned outdoor sofa and indicated she should join him there.

She took the far corner to give them some space.

"So tell me what you want," Vince said, dropping those shades back in place, covering his expression again.

"What do you mean?" she asked, stalling.

He said nothing. Just waited. What she wanted, what she *needed*, was help. She needed the project to save the family business, and she needed help doing that, but she didn't think he would easily hand over the project and then help her with it. She had to find a way to put it to him that made them both come out a winner.

Her cell rang in her purse, the ringtone the embarrassing "Living La Vida Loca" that her mom had programmed as her ringtone. It was never good news when her mom called.

She turned back to Vince. "I want to keep the historic original part of the library intact."

The cell finally went quiet. She'd call her mom back later at a more convenient, private time.

"Brick is expensive," Vince said. "If you want to add an entire new section in brick, *if* the council goes with your plan, it's going to raise the cost significantly."

"I might be able to counter that with tax credits for historic preservation. Something I'm looking into. I've already asked—"

"Living La Vida Loca" rang out again from her purse. She felt herself flush.

"You need to get that?"

"No, no. I'll call her back." She snatched the cell to turn it off when she noticed a new text: *You're going to be a big sister!*

She stared at the words. She already was a big sister. That was weird. Wait. No, no, no! She punched in her mom's number. "Mom! It's me. What do you mean I'm going to be a big sister?"

"What do you think, Soph?" her mom replied cheerily. "I'm expecting!"

Sophia's stomach dropped. She glanced back at Vince,

who was staring at her. She moved away from the back patio and started pacing in the grass. "Mom, is it Manuel's?"

"Who else?"

Her dad? Her mom had left with Manuel six weeks ago. She stopped pacing and whispered, "Are you sure it's not just menopause?"

"I'm forty-five. Is it so hard to believe your old mom got knocked up?" Sophia was twenty-six. Her mom had her at eighteen. It was possible she was pregnant, just a shock.

Sophia resumed pacing. Her dad was going to be devastated. "Are you sure? Have you seen a doctor?"

"Sure as a ripe old banana and mango coming together!" she sang. Whatever the hell that meant. "Aren't you going to congratulate us?"

"Congratulations, Mom."

"You still living in that old drafty house?"

"Yes, I'm still there."

"Tell your dad to put it on the market. I'm not coming back."

"You tell him, Mom."

"Oh, I would, but he's so difficult to talk to. Always cutting me off. He doesn't want to listen."

Sophia's shoulders slumped. Her dad was loud, domineering, and muleheaded, but ever since her mom had left, he'd been a shell of his former self. She really did fear this was the last nail in the coffin. "I'll try to talk to him about the house," she said. "You tell him about—" she lowered her voice "—the other thing."

"Gotta go! Give your brother a squeeze for me."

"He's—" Her mom hung up before she could tell her Mike was still touring with Mink Jewel. Well, not exactly touring, more like following them from one dive bar to another. She pressed her lips tightly together and returned to the patio. She sat and stared at the stone pattern, not really seeing it. Tears swam in her vision. Her family was falling apart and nobody seemed to care except her. Why was she trying so hard? Just give up. Give Vince the project, let Capello

Construction fold, make her brother work for once in his life, but then her dad…

"Everything okay?" Vince asked.

She nodded, her throat tight.

"Sophia," Vince said in that deep melodic way he had of making her name sound like a song.

She wiped an errant tear and squared her shoulders. "So. Where were we?"

"You're going to be a big sister?" he asked.

"Yes. Well." She ran out of words. She did not want to spill her family's dirty laundry to the man she was supposed to be impressing with Capello Construction.

"You're not happy about it?"

She couldn't answer.

Vince reached over and squeezed her shoulder. "Hey, you want to reschedule?"

She shook her head. "No. Of course not. The meeting is on Tuesday." Sweat broke out everywhere at once, and she felt light-headed as the enormity of the hole she was in crashed over her head. Her dad, already barely hanging on by a thread, was going to lose it when he heard about this pregnancy. He'd be no help to her at all. She didn't know what she was doing with Capello Construction. It was all going to end in a spectacular crash on her watch. If she didn't win the project, they were finished. There was nothing like it on the horizon that could pull them out of debt. If she did win the project, she'd still lose because she didn't know where to begin with a construction crew, and she didn't have time anyway. She still had her own job. Barely.

The answer sitting across from her in shades only added to her distress. How was she supposed to get Marino Construction to work with Capello Construction with their history? Why would they want to? They wouldn't.

She was screwed. Her family was screwed. Forty-two years of family business gone before it could get to the next generation, her brother.

Nausea welled up, and she leaped from her seat. "Can I use your bathroom?"

"Sure."

She ran straight to the small powder room she'd seen off the kitchen, hung her head over the sink, and tried to breathe normally. She ran the faucet and splashed cold water on her face. The nausea passed. She took a few deep breaths.

She patted her face dry with a hand towel that looked like it had never been used. She stared at her reflection as the only viable solution, a partnership with Marino Construction, settled more firmly in her mind. Maybe this could be a good thing. Maybe she and Vince could be the voice of reason in this long-running feud between their families. Maybe they could call a halt to the insanity that had only hurt both family businesses. She honestly didn't see any alternative at this point. They were two days away from the town council's decision. She would be the bigger person and offer an equitable partnership between them. That way she wasn't asking for help, merely offering a sharing of the work. And hopefully Vince would take over directing the construction crew on his own, as he seemed the kind of man used to taking charge. That settled, and feeling much calmer, she returned to the patio and took her seat.

"You okay?" he asked.

"I'm fine, thank you," she replied cordially. "So, how about, whichever way the council decides, we split the work among our two crews fifty-fifty?"

"Like hell," he said.

"I have a huge crew waiting for work—"

"Me too," Vince thundered. "What you seem to be conveniently forgetting here is that I put months of work into this project already."

"My family really needs this," she said quietly.

"Look, I don't know your family's trouble, and I don't want to know. I'm taking over Marino and Sons, and this is the project that keeps us going for the next year." He leaned forward, elbows resting on his knees. "So what's it going to take to make Capello Construction go away?"

"You mean me?" Rage began a slow boil within her. She

hadn't come this far just to walk away. Her family needed her. Hell, she was their very last hope.

"It's obvious your family's in some sort of crisis. You don't know what the hell you're doing. How much?"

She knew exactly how much she needed. The exact amount her dad had spent on the alpaca farm in Virginia in a misguided attempt to win her mom back. Because, of course, her mom had once remarked that alpacas were cute. The farm had been on the market for three years before her dad bought it, and now that it was back on the market, nobody wanted it. For some ridiculous reason, her dad had thought retiring hundreds of miles away on an isolated farm would keep his wife from being tempted away from him. Wrong in so many ways. Her mom was a social butterfly and, as she'd unfortunately shared with Sophia, reaching her "sexual peak." But Manuel would know all about that.

"One million dollars," Sophia said.

"Ha!" Vince whipped off his shades. "You're crazy, lady."

"I'm dead serious. You want me out? That's what will get me out. Otherwise, I'll see you on Tuesday, and I have a feeling it's going to go my way."

She stood and grabbed her purse. She couldn't believe she'd been ogling him. He was not on her side. He wasn't going to help her. So much for being the bigger person. No wonder their families hated each other. The Marinos were completely unreasonable and difficult. She had to do this on her own, just like everything else in her life.

He stood, crossing his massive arms, his legs braced apart like he was going into battle. "Why would they pick you? For a damn historic plaque? File some freaking paperwork? Anyone could do that! Just get out while you can before everyone finds out you don't know what the hell you're doing!"

She narrowed her eyes and threw his words back in his face. "Like hell."

A ghost of a smile crossed his face, and he leaned closer, his eyes burning into hers. "This isn't about you, Sophia. From what I can tell, you're a good girl trying to do right, but

I'm telling you this isn't your fight. And you sure as hell don't want to be in it with me." He smirked.

"I can't believe I kissed you," she spat.

He leaned back. "Didn't do much for me either."

Her gut twisted. "I take back every nice thought I ever had about you."

One corner of his mouth lifted. "I'm surprised you had more than one. Then again, I did save that pretty little ass of yours."

She sputtered, unsure if she should take a swing at him or just save all that rage and funnel it into obliterating him at the meeting.

"You're welcome," he added.

Her hands were in fists. "My father hates your company and, if you're any indication, he has good reason."

"My father hates your company too." He nodded sagely. "We're like the fucking Montagues and Capulets."

She lifted her chin. "I've got news for you, Vince, you are not my Romeo."

And with that she made her big exit. Her cell rang again, but the Sinatra "My Way" ringtone from her dad wasn't nearly loud enough to drown out Vince's bark of laughter.

～

Sophia drove straight to her uncle Phil's house in Queens to visit her dad and make him help her. Her dad answered the door in a bathrobe and slippers. He was unshaven and had deep bags under his eyes. His salt-and-pepper hair was disheveled, thin, and greasy. She suppressed a sigh of frustration.

"Did you hear about your mother?" he asked on a moan.

"Yes, Dad," she said gently. "I heard."

"Do you think she's just yanking my chain?"

She looked around the small living room littered with empty pizza boxes, beer cans, cheese puffs, and a nearly empty bottle of scotch, and immediately set to work cleaning up. "Where's Uncle Phil?"

"He went to Florida on my behalf."

Sophia froze, her hands full of pizza boxes. "You sent Uncle Phil to talk to Mom?"

Her dad flopped into a worn recliner. "I didn't send him. He wanted to go."

"Why?"

He shrugged, picked up a beer can from the floor and drank. "I think he's trying to get rid of me."

"Dad, you can come home. You don't have to hide. We'll replace the money. I've got this library project. By Tuesday, I should hear something. We can still fix this."

"I can't go back to Greenport. Your mother made that impossible. You think I don't know what they're saying about me? That I've been replaced by the pool boy? They're snickering, saying I need the Viagra."

Sophia closed her eyes, torn between a laugh and a scream. "No one is saying that."

What they were saying was why did Joe Capello think buying his wife an alpaca farm in Virginia was going to make her stay?

She headed to the kitchen for a garbage bag.

"They're thinking it!" he hollered after her. He grumbled some more stuff she couldn't quite catch and didn't ask him to repeat.

She returned to the small living room and started stuffing all the trash into the garbage bag. Something moved, darting between the paper plates. "Ahh!" She startled, heart pounding. It was a cockroach. The thing skittered away. She shuddered.

"Soph, geez, keep the noise down." He hit the remote on the TV.

Sophia yanked the TV's plug out of the wall.

"Hey!"

She stood in front of him, staring him down. "You need to take a shower, get dressed, and help me save this freaking company, or I swear it's all going down the toilet! Marino and Sons is not backing off. In fact, I think they're going to get the whole project, historic structure or not. Vince is pissed—"

"Vinny's boy?"

"Dad, wake up!" she shouted. "Yes! The one you warned me about! Why am I even helping you?"

He crossed his arms.

She lowered her voice and said as calmly as possible, "Dad, you know I love you, and I know you're going through a difficult time, but if you don't help me at least a little, that's it. There's nothing more I can do." She shook her head sadly. Then she said the two little words she knew would light a fire under him. "Marino wins."

"Fine!" He heaved a sigh and pushed out of the chair, muttering about Marino under his breath. "I'm taking a shower and then we'll come up with a plan of attack."

"Thank you."

Her dad stopped in front of her on his way out, love shining in his eyes. "But if anyone can take him, it's you." He patted her cheek. "You've got the Capello fire."

"I'm not so sure that's a good thing," she said, feeling defeated. She felt like she was always fighting and never getting anywhere.

"Of course it's good! Make me some coffee, would ya?"

She nodded and returned to cleaning up, carefully picking up each item with two fingers as she cringed, hoping not to make contact with another cockroach.

An hour later, she sat across the kitchen table from her dad, clean-shaven, and looking more like his old self. "I know Vince," her dad said. "He's just as bad as his dad, am I right?"

"I don't know! I never met his dad. Maybe you should do the presentation on Tuesday." She would love to avoid seeing Vince again. He got her so worked up. She didn't even feel like herself around him. She turned into a swearing, kiss-stealing ogler. That was so not her.

"I'm not ready to go back to work," her dad said forlornly. "You don't know what it's like to have the love of your life just up and leave you."

"I'm sorry, Dad," she said gently.

"Do you think she's coming back?" he asked, pathetically hopeful.

She answered honestly, as she always did with this question. "No, I don't."

He sipped his coffee. Then he set the mug down and dropped his head in his hands.

She couldn't let him descend back into that dark place. She needed him focused. "Vince is so obnoxious. I'll bet his dad's like that too."

Her dad's head jerked up. "His dad was always so full of himself, so confident. All charm and flash."

She nodded knowingly. "Like father, like son. Dad, I could really use you there on Tuesday. My construction background isn't nearly as strong as yours."

He waved that away. "My crew knows what to do. I have every confidence." He sipped his coffee. "Does the town council like Vince?"

She brushed some crumbs off the table and into her hand, standing to throw them away. "Probably. But they were willing to listen to me."

"That's good. See, I knew putting you in there would be helpful."

She sat down again. "Vince keeps going on about how your design costs a lot more, and he's got a point. Why would they want to pay more?"

"I thought you said we could get some tax credits."

"It's not that much money, and it's not guaranteed. He says the brick surround I wanted to match the historic structure is too much."

"So we'll just do a brick front." He yawned and sipped more coffee. "We do that all the time for houses."

"That would look terrible."

"Nah. People don't care."

"I care."

"Just do some fundraising. Get people in town to cough up the dough." He pointed at her. "Tell the mayor that."

"I got the feeling they wanted to break ground and get moving as quickly as possible. Marino and Sons can do that."

He pounded the table with his fist. "Do they want it done fast, or do they want it done right?"

Not the first time she'd heard that from him. It was his standard answer to impatient clients. "So no compromise? Just do it our way and find a way to pay for it."

"Exactly."

"Are you sure you can't come to the meeting? I think Vince wouldn't argue with you as much as with me."

Her dad stiffened. "Is he being disrespectful to my little girl?"

She heaved a sigh. "He—" She stopped. Vince had saved her. He'd given her a tour of his house, knowing her interest in it. He'd tried to have a nice dinner before they talked business. Why had she gotten so mad at him? Something about Vince just got under her skin. "No, he's fine. Just difficult."

Her dad scoffed. "Difficult. Of course he's difficult. He's Vinny's boy. You give him hell, Soph." He mimed strangling someone. "Go for the jugular."

She stood. "I'm not going to give him hell. I'm going to go into the meeting as a professional and hope they come around to our idea." She watched as her dad got another cup of coffee. "Dad, please come home. Sleeping on Uncle Phil's couch is no way to live." She'd understood at first why her dad had wanted to crash there, avoiding town gossip about his errant wife with the pool boy and his outrageous mistake with the alpaca farm, but by now surely the gossip had turned to other more interesting topics. Seriously, enough was enough.

He waved that away. She crossed to him and kissed him on the cheek. He smelled like Old Spice, the aftershave he'd been using since she was a kid. "I'll let you know how it goes."

"Thanks, Soph. I knew I could count on you. Unlike your brother. What the hell is he up to?"

She backed away. "Bye, Dad."

He was still grumbling about college tuition and stupidity when she left.

7

Vince tried to put a pleasant expression on his face as he waited in the Clover Park Library meeting room for the big decision. Sophia wasn't here yet. The mayor and town council were talking amongst themselves about the possibility of a town-wide talent show as a fundraiser. He would've been tense anyway, waiting to hear the final decision, but then his dad had to show up at work to check up on him right before the meeting. Again. Vince had finally told him about the Capello proposal, which resulted in an angry tirade and a final "Don't screw this up." Vince had been tagging along to work meetings with his dad for years; he knew how to act. If he didn't get this damn promotion, he didn't know what he'd do. He was beginning to think his dad would never take him seriously.

He knew the moment she entered the room, as all conversation stopped at the vision before them—Sophia in a dress that looked like fire, all shades of red and orange, the flames licking upward. The dress went up to her chin in a turtleneck, tight at the waist with a thin black belt, and fluffy layers on the skirt. But the kicker, what made his pants feel a size too small, were ridiculously high-heeled black leather boots that stopped just below her bare knees.

"Hello, gentlemen," she called as she walked to the head of the table. "How are you?"

The gentlemen scrambled to answer her, talking over each other. Vince's eyes traveled up to her smiling face. Her hair was up, revealing bare earlobes, no earrings. She didn't need jewelry to frame that face. That beautiful—

She met his eyes and smirked. He slowly shook his head. If she thought for one minute he was going to be taken in by a pretty face, he had news for her. He eased out of his chair and crossed to her side.

"Aren't you a vision?" he whispered just for her ears.

She smiled tightly and continued taking papers out of a small portfolio case. "Thank you."

"Looks don't get the job done."

"I suppose that's good news for you," she said quietly, "seeing as how you look like you stepped out of an L.L.Bean catalog."

He chuckled. "What're you talking about?"

"You're built like a lumberjack. Like an L.L.Bean model minus the flannel."

The remark meant to sting warmed him. He hadn't known she looked at him as anything but annoying. Sure she'd kissed him, but that had been more like a grateful damsel-in-distress thing. She'd point-blank said that he was not her Romeo. He leaned close, getting a whiff of her spicy rose scent that made him want to inhale deep. "You into me, Juliet?"

She blinked slowly and then shuffled her papers. "Take your seat. I'm about to school you."

"If you were my teacher, I might've paid more attention."

Her lips twitched, but then she pursed them together, unwilling to smile for him. He kind of wanted to make her smile now, sort of felt cheated with the almost smile.

"Shall we begin?" Sophia asked, addressing the room. Her father hadn't shown up. So it was just the mayor, the six middle-aged horndogs on the town council, and him.

"Whenever you're ready," Mayor Riggs said, smoothing

the lock of long white hair he thought covered his huge bald spot.

"So Vince and I sat down to talk, and we came to the conclusion that my design—" she held up the brick design in front of her "—is more expensive. And might take a little more time." She looked at him and smiled sweetly, which made him nervous. What was she doing? She was making things worse for herself. "But I have the solution. Along with tax incentives for preserving the historic building, a fundraising campaign that really brings the town together."

"They have a fundraising campaign," Vince said.

"Go on," Mayor Riggs said. "Vince, you'll have your turn."

"Thank you," Sophia said. "We let donors see their name on the sidewalk and on a plaque in the entryway." She pointed out on her drawing where it would go. "Also, on a wall of sponsors on the lower level and on a giving tree artistically painted in the children's section. This brings pride of ownership to the building. And I know at least Mayor Riggs has been to one of my mother's fundraisers, a bachelor auction, and I seem to remember you went for a very high bid." She winked, and the mayor chuckled. "I can use my mother's connections to sponsor a series of fundraiser dinners, fashion shows, bachelor auctions, any or all of the above as long as it's fun."

She paused and the room was quiet, the men hanging on her every word. "It might mean a small delay in construction, a few months for historic designation and extra fundraising, but we are making history here. This library will stand for the next hundred years, pointing the way to the future as it preserves the past."

The room broke out in applause. Vince felt like howling. Instead he joined her at the head of the table. "Of course you can always raise more funds," he said in as calm a voice as he could muster. "But with this brick design, which is significantly more expensive, you lose the view of the park. The best part of this library is its location. This design completely ignores that."

"Could you add bigger windows, Sophia?" the mayor asked.

"Sure," Sophia responded.

Vince pulled out his design and tapped the various parts of the building. "Brick cannot replicate this. Floor-to-ceiling glass, light wood accents. This space is meant to be open, light, and airy, not a continuation of a design created more than a hundred years ago."

"This town has a long, proud history," Sophia said. "I understand that."

"I understand history," Vince said through clenched teeth.

Sophia kept going. "And I hope you know my father will be working closely with me on the project. He'll be directing the crew while I manage the historic preservation efforts. So with Capello Construction you get the best of both worlds—experienced construction and expert historic consulting."

"Where is Mr. Capello?" Vince asked. "We haven't seen him at any of these meetings. How do we know he'll show up?"

"He'll show," Sophia said between her teeth. She smiled for the benefit of the other men. "He's recovering from an illness. He will definitely be fine by the time we've raised the necessary funds."

Mayor Riggs rubbed his chin. "Hmm…tough decision. But after some thought, we have to say the idea of preserving the old library appeals to us. Clover Park has only a few historic spots left on Main Street. If you could add some more windows, Sophia, to capture that view out front, we'd really like to go with Capello Construction."

"Wait a minute," Vince said. "It's not that easy to just add windows with brick. You need strong supports, retaining walls—" He blew out a breath, beyond frustrated. He was going to lose it soon, and it wasn't going to be pretty. How did his dad deal with idiotic meetings like this?

Sophia put her hand on his arm. "I'll call my engineering department."

"I'm afraid we've made our decision, Vince," Mayor Riggs said. "We'll keep you in mind for the next project."

And with that, he was dismissed. Vince strode from the room, jaw clenched. He went outside and headed straight to the park. He couldn't drive when he was this furious. He couldn't believe how quickly they made their decision. They didn't even want to hear from him. Well, why would they? They already knew what he had to say. He'd been saying it for months already. So no big job. No promotion. Just more hard days working construction. His dad was right. Vince didn't have what it took to get the job done. He wasn't good enough.

He was not looking forward to that parental-boss conversation. He sat on a bench in the gazebo until the quiet of the park calmed him enough to head home. He strode across the street, heading to the parking lot. Sophia was sitting on a bench in front of the library. She jumped up when she saw him.

"Hi," she said.

He stopped short, looking to the sky for whatever patience might be offered from above and, receiving none, turned and blasted her. "Congratulations on killing my business and making everyone in town pay far more than they can afford all because you—" he gestured up and down her body "—sashay in with a pretty dress and a pretty face!"

She stopped in front of him, looking completely unruffled and calm, which just got him more worked up. "Thank you. You want to grab a bite?"

"What I want," he growled, getting in her face, "is to bite your head off."

"I would taste terrible. Too much hair product. Follow me. I have a proposal for you."

She was entirely too pleasant for the level of rage he was feeling. "You're proposing?" he barked.

"Yes, Vince, I would love to be your wife." She rolled her eyes. "Come on." She kept going, stopping by her damn Mini Cooper.

"I'm not getting in that thing again," he said. "It looks like a toy."

"Fine. We'll take your car." She looked around. "Which

one is it? Oh, wait, let me guess. The muscle car." She pointed over at his Camaro. "Am I right?"

He wasn't going anywhere with her. "Everything is screwed up!" he boomed. "I'm probably going to have to quit my job—"

"No! Don't quit. Just grab a bite and listen to me."

He headed over to his car, and she hurried alongside him. He turned. "Leave me alone."

She put her hand on his arm. "Please! I'll make it worth your while. I promise."

She sounded desperate. He stopped. "You promise?"

She blew out a breath. "Yes."

"What if I don't think it's worth my while?"

A beat passed while she thought it over. This should be good. "Then I'll let you kick my ass," she said with a nod. "I know you want to."

"Let me—" He scrubbed a hand over his face. "Geez, you're demented. I would never hurt a woman." He headed for his car and unlocked it.

She appeared at his side, looking up at him with big puppy eyes. The eyes and the sexpot body made it tough to hang onto his mad. "What, then?" she asked. "What would make it worth your while?"

"Nothing."

Her hand was on his arm again. The spicy rose scent wrapped around him. "Vince, please."

He glanced down at her hand. "Are you begging me?"

"Yes, I am begging you."

"You're in over your head, aren't you?"

She nodded.

"Too bad." He got into the car and turned the ignition. The passenger door opened. He dropped his forehead to the steering wheel. Would this day never end?

"I'm grabbing a bite with you," she said, fastening her seatbelt. "And then we'll talk."

He let out a noisy breath. Like she gave him much choice, other than physically removing her from his car. He eyed her, sitting there in that flaming red dress, bare knees and a bit of thigh showing. The idea had merit. He'd get to touch her and toss her.

"You can't kick me out!" she exclaimed, gripping the seat tightly. "I'll just follow you in my car until you listen!"

He raised a brow. "Fine. I'll get food with you." She sounded just desperate enough that he thought maybe he could still salvage the project.

She immediately started ordering him around, giving him directions to where she wanted to grab a bite. He felt a muscle tick in his cheek. He was used to giving orders, not taking them. Especially not tonight when she'd stolen the business right out from under him.

"Are you done?" he asked.

"If my directions were clear, then yes."

"We're going to Burger Shack." She might be in his car, she might be insisting on prolonging this night with a damn proposal, but he'd be damned if they weren't going where he wanted.

She smiled sunnily. "Perfect! I love burgers."

He deflated. He just could not win with her.

He put the car in gear and peeled out of there. Now his car was going to smell like her, all sex and roses. Sophia fiddled with the radio, annoying him as she tried to find a song she liked. Finally a song he liked came on, and she started singing along. Great. She even had to ruin that. Now he'd never hear this song again without hearing her sultry voice. He loosened his tie. Damn, he was so screwed. In every sense of the word. All because of this crazy, ridiculously appealing woman.

Sophia walked through the door of Burger Shack that Vince held open for her, working on not noticing the way his thick dark brown hair was sexily rumpled like he'd run his hands through it. Or the way his eyes were at half-mast, which gave him a hooded, sexy look, but was probably a result of him checking out her bare legs right this very minute. She'd seen him eyeing her knees in the car. And she definitely didn't notice the way he filled out that shirt. He'd left his tie and suit jacket on the backseat of his car. Why was she so obsessed with his size? Yes, he was a large man built like a lumberjack. That had nothing to do with her purpose here tonight. She had no idea if her dad would ever get his shit together and take the lead on this project. There were many employees depending on it, on her. And she still had her own job, and her boss wasn't happy about all the time off she'd had to take. She couldn't be running a construction crew. More importantly, she didn't know how. She turned to the one man who could help save the project and her father's company and said, "Grab us a table. I'll get the food. My treat."

His dark brown eyes burned into hers. "Oh, really. Your treat. How generous."

She shrugged. "It's a business expense."

He crossed his arms in front of his chest, making his biceps bulge. "You don't even know what I want."

"Double burger, medium rare, large fries, and bottled water."

He uncrossed his arms and stared at her. "Did you do some research on me?"

"Not at all." She turned back around, moving up with the line, and said over her shoulder, "You're very easy to read. Big hefty guy likes red meat and lots of fries."

She faced front, heard some heavy breathing behind her, but no response. She glanced over a moment later to find he'd grabbed them a table. Step one in reaching a palatable compromise, let your opponent know who was in charge. She ordered herself the same, paid for both meals, and joined him at the table.

Vince took a big bite of his burger, chewed, and swallowed it down. "One, I'm not hefty and two, I gotta tell ya, ordering a guy around doesn't make him want to listen to much more of what you've got to say."

"No?" She took a fry and dipped it in his paper cup of ketchup.

He shifted the ketchup out of her reach.

She took a bite of burger and chewed. Took another bite.

"Okay, what?" he snapped. "What is this proposal of yours? Just spit it out."

She held up a finger, finished chewing, and wiped her mouth with a napkin. "Don't you want to eat?"

"I'm rapidly losing my appetite."

She picked up a fry and pointed to his ketchup with it. "Could I just…" He let out a heavy sigh and pushed the ketchup toward her. She bit back a smile. Step two in reaching a palatable compromise, make your opponent give you something.

She dipped another fry in his ketchup and took a bite.

"Sophia," he growled, "I am this close to walking out of here."

"But you won't," she replied. She unscrewed the cap on her bottled water and took a sip.

"What do you want?" he said through his teeth. "Just tell me so I can tell you no and get out of here."

"What's the rush?" she asked, taking another bite of burger. After she chewed, she added, "I thought you liked burgers. You're the one who wanted to come here."

He scowled and took a bite of his burger.

She smiled. "Good, right?"

He grunted. Step three in reaching a palatable compromise—find common ground. They were both enjoying their double medium-rare burgers.

Then she remembered what he said the last time they'd shared a meal and reminded him. "I want to enjoy my meal without any indigestion, *capisce*?"

He stood. "Let's go."

"Vince, I'm not done eating."

He snagged her burger, strode over to the garbage, and tossed it in. "Done."

He returned to the table, glowering down at her from his full six-foot-something height. She grabbed his burger and took a big bite, nearly choking on it. She coughed and her eyes watered, but she managed to keep it in.

He slammed his hands on his hips. "You are a piece of work, lady."

"I know," she said around the burger.

He barked out a laugh. She laughed too and spit some pickle. He handed her a napkin. "You drive me crazy, you know that?"

She nodded, still working on chewing the burger.

He sat down again and grabbed a fry. "Pass the ketchup."

They ended up sharing what was left of his burger. She figured sharing food was as close as she was ever going to get to him, so she launched right into her proposal as soon as they finished.

"What I'm thinking is, you know construction, you know how to get the job done—"

"Thank you!" Vince boomed. "This is what I've been saying."

"So I'm proposing a merger of Capello Construction and Marino and Sons. I could create a historic architecture department that I would lead, and you could lead the new construction of both companies. We could add significantly to your client list. We've done commercial work and a lot of residential new construction. I know you haven't broken into the residential sector yet. What do you think?"

He leaned back and let out a low whistle. "Does your dad know about this?"

"It was his idea."

He slapped a hand on the table. "No fucking way. What are you trying to pull here?"

"Okay, okay, it wasn't his idea. It's mine. It's the only way I can see for Capello Construction to stay afloat."

He scowled. "Riding on my coffers."

"Maybe it's time to end all this hostility between our families. The way our fathers compete, underbidding the projects just to win—"

"Your dad's the one who always lowballs us," Vince retorted.

"Either way," she said diplomatically. "Their competing hasn't helped either business in the long run. I know I'll have to let some of our guys go, but maybe I can bring in enough new business on the restoration of historic buildings that I could bring them back. Soon, I hope."

"What the hell's going on with your dad and this company? Why would you want this?" He fixed her with a hard stare. "Be straight with me."

She looked around the restaurant. They were in Eastman, only one town over from Clover Park, but she didn't see anyone she knew from the library project. She gestured him closer. He leaned in, and she started to whisper her explanation.

He shook his head. "I can't hear you that well. Too much noise in here. Let's go back to the car."

The car was his space. They needed neutral territory. She got up, walked over to his side, and sat next to him on the bench seat.

"You don't take direction well, do you?" he asked.

She stared straight ahead and spoke out of the corner of her mouth. "Promise you won't tell anyone what I'm about to say."

He let out a noisy sigh. "Should we pinky swear?"

She turned to him. "Promise!"

He rolled his eyes. "Fine." He slid a little further down the bench seat, leaving some space between them.

She closed the gap, pressing up against his side to confess.

"Gimme a little space here," Vince said, sounding aggrieved. "You're practically in my lap."

"I don't want anyone to hear."

"Which is why I suggested the car."

He shifted away again until he was against the wall. She started talking in a low voice, casually leaning closer so her voice wouldn't carry. "My dad took a million dollars from the company, and we're on the verge of bankruptcy. That's why we needed this project so badly."

He hissed out a breath. "I can't believe you would steal this project, knowing this. How were you planning on keeping the whole thing going? You know they don't just give you the whole amount up front. It's in payments as work is completed."

"I was still working on that part."

He muttered a curse and shook his head. "Why didn't you just let me have the project and ask to join in?"

She scoffed. "You'd never take us on once the project was yours. Now it's mine, and I can share."

"You can share," he echoed. "This is nuts."

"It's still a good deal for you," she insisted. "We have a great reputation. Lots of contacts and clients. It's just a tempo-rary cash-flow problem."

"What would your dad say about all this?"

"He put me in charge. He's gone off the deep end. My brother was supposed to take over the company, but he has no interest in it. I'm sure he wouldn't care. He's a groupie for a punk rock band."

He gave her a sideways look. "I need to think it over."

She pressed up against his side, ignoring how hot and tingly it made her. She wasn't letting him out of the booth without an answer. "Think fast."

"Would you like to sit in my lap?" he asked.

She lifted her chin. "I'm not letting you out of this booth until I know if you're for or against my proposal."

"Moving you is not a problem."

She crossed her arms, working on being an immovable force.

He let out a noisy breath. "How many do you have on payroll?"

"A hundred, give or take."

He shook his head. "You're going to have to let more than half go. I've got seventy on my side, and I can't keep both crews on payroll."

"So you'll do it? You'll merge us?" When he didn't respond, she added in a soft voice, "Save us?"

He pressed his lips in a flat line and slid her a foot away. "I can't believe I only got half of a lipsticked burger out of this deal."

She bounced a little in her seat. "So you'll do it?"

He gave her a hard look. "It's not that simple. Our dads have to sign off on it. Lawyers have to get involved. This kind of thing takes time. I need to look over your books, meet your crew, get all up in your business, *capisce*?"

"*Capisce*." She licked her lips, and the next words felt like they were wrenched from her throat. "Thank you."

He raised a brow. "Don't thank me yet. It's far from definite. We have to handle this delicately, or we'll have an all-out war on our hands with the old guys."

"My dad can be a pit bull."

"My dad is a bulldog."

"So what should we do about the library project?"

"We?" he asked in a tone that said he knew he had the upper hand.

"Well, yeah." She swallowed hard, extremely uncomfortable with him having the upper hand. "I thought—"

"Ya know what? That's a good place to start. The library will be a trial project. A test run, so to speak. The way I see it, I'm in charge. I'll take on thirty of your guys and you, the rest is Marino and Sons. Our name right alongside yours at that groundbreaking ceremony. You won't recoup a million up front, but by the end of the project you'll have it plus you'll have kept thirty of your best guys employed." He paused. "Do you know who your best guys are?"

She wanted to say *you. You are my best guy right now*. But instead she shrugged one shoulder. "The guys that have been with us longest stay."

He frowned. "You got a bunch of old geezers over there, don't you?"

She was in no position to demand anything, and she knew it.

"They stay or the deal's off," she said.

One corner of his mouth lifted. "You got some balls on you." He laughed. "I'm going to have fun with you."

She lifted her chin. "What's that supposed to mean?"

He placed a finger under her chin, holding it there. "Gimme a kiss to seal the deal."

Her heart hammered against her rib cage. "I will not."

"We have to seal the deal somehow," he said. "Besides you

got me a little worked up the way you sat in my lap and offered me a huge job. Kinda turned my night around."

She huffed. "I did not sit in your lap." She slapped his finger away. "You said my kiss didn't do anything for you." The words still stung.

He smirked, but his large warm hand cupped her cheek, and her eyes closed on their own. "It's for you," he said.

Her eyes flew open. "You are so full of yourself!"

He gave her a devious knowing smile. "Let's go, partner."

She frowned and grabbed her purse.

He broke into a wide smile. "I like when you follow orders."

That did it. "Listen, I don't care if you're the only life vest in this hell I found myself in, I don't take orders from anyone!"

He turned her and said in a low voice, "Move it."

She stayed stock-still to prove her point. No order taking here. His arm snaked around her waist and then he lifted her, tucking her like a football against his hip, and carried her out. Her cheeks flamed as people in the crowded restaurant stared, mouths open. She wanted to kick and scream, but she was wearing a dress. "Put me down," she hissed.

He whistled on the way to the car. Then he set her down by the passenger side and opened her door for her. "Get in."

She crossed her arms. "How dare you! I won't—"

His voice rumbled in her ear, low and dangerous. "Easy way or the hard way?"

She flushed and got in the car. As soon as they pulled into the street, she let him have it. "Don't you ever lay a hand on me again!"

He glanced at her. "Damn, if you could see yourself now. Your cheeks are pink, your eyes dilated, your breathing is coming a little harder. I think you like my hands on you."

"Think again!"

He stopped at a red light and his eyes met hers with an unholy gleam. "Can I be honest?"

She licked her lips. "What?"

"Strictly between us, forget all that work stuff—" he waved that away "—from one sexy beast to another…"

She choked on a laugh. "Continue."

One corner of his mouth lifted. "I'd bet good money your pansy-ass boyfriends never give you what you need."

She gripped the edge of her seat. "And what exactly do you think I need?"

"You need someone to take charge, someone that gets you out of your head and makes you…" He stopped and turned back to face the road, the words just hanging there.

"Makes me what?" She was suddenly desperate to find out what she needed because Vince was right. Her past boyfriends always left her unsatisfied.

He hit the accelerator and turned the radio on, driving along as if he'd lost interest in the conversation.

She stewed for a few minutes, then finally turned the radio off. "Makes me what? You have to finish your sentence."

"Nah. I'm done messing with you." He slapped the steering wheel. "Back to business."

"Just one more minute with the sexy beast. Tell me!"

He chuckled; then he dropped his voice, low and seductive. "Makes you let go."

"I-I…oh." His hungry gaze made her almost forget the position she was in. She needed to work with him, to make their businesses work together.

At her silence, he asked, "When was the last time you lost control?"

Never. Never was the last time. She was the strong capable one that ran around fixing things for everyone else— her family, her friends, her pansy-ass boyfriends.

She swallowed hard. "This conversation is ridiculous. I'm sorry I made you finish that stupid sexy-beast sentence." She gripped the edge of her seat tighter. "And, by the way, I'm not into being carried around like a football."

His voice was low, scraping her insides, making everything tighten. "Tell me what you're into."

She forced her fingers to let go of the seat, feigning indifference. "I'm fine, thank you."

She never should've indulged in this inappropriately hot conversation. Obviously, Vince had called her sexy just to lure her down the seduction path. He was a player. She knew it the moment she laid eyes on that lumberjack body. If she ever slept with him, which she wouldn't, he'd be out of there so fast the sheets would still be burning.

What would that be like? Burning up the sheets. She looked out the window, away from his massive hand casually controlling the steering wheel.

She didn't need him for that. She met nice men all the time. Men that weren't so physical, so in your face, so rough around the edges. Rugged. Strong. The throbbing between her legs was a major distraction. Vince was out of line, and it was time to put him back in his place, especially with the way he was cheerfully whistling right now like he wasn't hot and bothered by this conversation at all. Probably just another day at the office for him.

"I've got your number," he said.

A thrill went through her. Did he? Did he really know what even she hadn't realized she craved, until now?

"You mean my phone number," she said to clarify.

"If it makes you feel better to think that." He turned the radio back on and found a station with a hard, pounding bass beat that matched the throbbing between her legs.

It was a short drive back to the library parking lot, where she'd left her car, and she debated continuing the outrageous, but intriguing sexy-beast conversation even as common sense told her to drop it. He wasn't all that. Just because he looked like an Italian lumberjack straight from an L.L.Bean catalog didn't mean he was any different from any other man. He was bluffing. He couldn't possibly know her or what she wanted. She barely knew that about herself.

She bit her lip as he pulled up next to her car. It was dark, but she always parked by a streetlight and it lit up one side of his face. He was so beautiful—chiseled cheekbones, full lips, a strong nose and jaw. The other side of his face in shadow—dark and mysterious. She was tempted, so tempted.

"Well, goodnight," she said in a cheery tone as if she wasn't damp and throbbing and craving. Omigod, the craving. She got out of the car in a hurry, and he got out too, walking with her to her car. She pretended not to notice him, got out her key, and struggled to unlock the car door. Her stupid hand was shaking, jittery at his proximity.

"Sophia."

She didn't want to turn around. She was afraid she'd cave. This was wrong, wrong, wrong.

His hand connected with her bottom gently, and she squeaked. He did a slow, sensual up and down stroke, and her knees went weak as the throbbing became more insistent. "Sorry if I spoke out of turn," he said. "Friends?"

She nodded automatically, unable to speak when all she could think to say was *more, please.*

"We'll call that sealing the deal," he said with a smile in his voice. Probably a smirk too.

She whirled. No way in hell they were sealing the deal with a butt rub. "You've got some nerve!"

He grinned. "I knew you'd be fun." Then he backed away, still grinning all cocky-like. "See you soon, partner."

8

———————

Vince showed up at his parents' house in Eastman for Sunday family dinner prepared to act the part of diplomat. He knew his dad wouldn't be keen on working with Capello Construction, to put it mildly, but from where Vince was standing, it was a valid business decision. He'd told his dad he'd gotten the job, and he'd be bringing the papers today. What he hadn't told him was that they were the subcontractor. Sophia had gotten everything in writing from the town, naming Marino and Sons as their subcontractor, and signed the papers on behalf of Capello Construction. Vince couldn't sign because he still wasn't full partner. That rankled, but he hoped his dad would see that he'd earned it. He'd salvaged the library project and, if things went well with the library project, a merger of the two companies could also be good for business. They'd take out their main competitor, making bidding on projects easier. Plus they'd make some headway into residential development and even get into historic places. Once the details were worked out, a merger could work very well for them going forward.

He'd given a lot of thought to what Sophia had said about ending the hostilities between the two families and finally concluded she was right. Did he really want to be responsible for continuing the feud down another generation? That was no way to run a business, especially in this competitive, but lucrative market. Though he knew better than to bring that up with his dad. He didn't want to hear another tirade about the horrible Joe Capello. He knew the man was aggressive and lowballed them, but at least now they had a solution to that problem. If he could make his dad listen long enough to hear reason. A stretch where Capello was concerned.

His petite blond stepmother answered the door. "Vince, so glad you could make it."

"How're ya, Ma?" He leaned down to kiss her cheek.

"I'm good. Better now that my boys are coming home."

"Everyone coming today?"

"As far as I know."

"Good." Vince figured he'd bring up the partnership idea in front of his family so his dad wouldn't fly off the handle. Especially if his new daughter-in-law, Zoe, was there. His dad was crazy about Zoe.

"Is that Vincent?" his dad hollered from the other room.

"Yeah, it's me." Vince followed the voice to the kitchen, where his dad quickly returned a beer to the fridge, looking guilty. "One beer won't kill ya."

His dad shook his head. "Your stepmom's been watching me like a hawk. I'm done with chemo, but she's a little on edge about my diet."

Vince understood. They'd all had a real scare when his dad had been diagnosed with stage three colon cancer, but the docs were hopeful that he was in the clear. He felt kinda bad for him having to sneak his favorite drink. He took a seat in the living room, where he was joined shortly by Gabe and Zoe, who his parents made a big fuss over on account of the grandchild-to-be.

"How's little Vince?" he asked.

Zoe beamed. "We picked a name, but we're not telling you all until after he's born."

"And it's not Vince," Gabe put in.

"What's wrong with Vincent?" his dad asked. "Good enough for me and this guy." He hooked a thumb in Vince's direction. Vince was a Junior.

"Vincent the third," Vince said. "Has a nice ring to it."

"That'll be your kid," Gabe said.

Vince scoffed. Like he'd ever get married. He got bored quickly and couldn't imagine being tied down to one woman his whole life like Gabe. He watched his brother for a moment, his hand on Zoe's stomach, whispering something to the baby. Vince's chest ached, and he rubbed it absentmindedly. Zoe giggled. He couldn't resist going over to put in his two cents to the baby.

"How ya doing, big guy?" he asked. "It's your uncle Vince, your godfather."

"Ooh, he kicked!" Zoe said, eyes wide. "I think he recognizes your voice."

"Course he does," Vince said. "I can't wait to teach you to throw a pass. And catch. You're going to be a prodigy on account of me."

Zoe smiled. "You'll make a good dad."

He raised a brow. "I'll make a good godfather. That's not the same thing."

"You seeing anyone?" Zoe asked. "Maybe I could set you up with a friend."

Gabe chuckled, and Vince shot him a dark look. "I don't need any help meeting someone. Thanks anyway."

Nico walked in with Angel. "It's not meeting someone Vince needs help with," Nico said with a smirk. "It's keeping them."

He socked Nico on the arm and grinned. "Like you should talk." Nico was nearly his height, though not built for football like Vince and their dad, with short dark brown hair and dark brown eyes. Women fell all over themselves for Nico, especially when he smiled. The wicked player smile with a touch of charm was a look his brother had perfected as a teen in front of the mirror.

"By choice, man," Nico said.

"How you feeling, Dad?" Angel asked. His youngest brother was lean with hardly any muscle and a good five inches shorter than Vince. He had the angelic demeanor of a priest with wavy dark brown hair, soft brown eyes, and a dimpled smile. It was surprising to everyone that he hadn't become one. Instead he was a social worker. He helped a lot of people for very little pay. Angel always said the work itself was reward enough.

"Fine, fine," their dad said. "Angel, come help me in the kitchen. I'm making chicken marsala."

"I'll help too," Zoe said, following them into the kitchen. Their mom followed Zoe in, chatting away with her.

"How's the library project going?" Gabe asked Vince. "Still butting heads with the supermodel?"

"What's this?" Nico asked. "You got a supermodel?" He gave Vince a one-two punch to the gut. "Good for you! Does she have a sister? Or better yet, a twin?"

Nico was such a horndog. Worse than Vince.

Vince elbowed Nico. "There's no supermodel." But she is beautiful, he added silently. His mind wandered to the last time he'd seen Sophia, how she'd gotten a little worked up, all pink-cheeked and flustered. He hadn't missed her hand shaking when she'd tried to unlock her car door. The feel of her curvy ass. He shouldn't have touched her. She'd gotten him worked up a bit, pressing up against him in that booth, and he'd wanted to turn the tables and put her in her place. Instead he'd gotten even more worked up. A problem he had to take care of solo once he got home.

But it wasn't just her looks, or the chemistry that he could tell went both ways. The more time he spent with her, the more he liked her. She was fun to spar with, she was smart, and, like him, she had a strong loyalty to family, however screwed up they were. This liking-the-enemy's-daughter problem wasn't going away, and while he would normally follow his lustful impulses, he knew, just knew, it would screw things up for him business-wise. His dad didn't take him seriously as it was; if he found out he'd slept with the person they were supposed to be doing business with, and his arch-rival's daughter to boot, he'd never be trusted to take over the company.

"Library project is getting there," Vince told Nico. "I'm going to talk to Dad about it at dinner."

Jared walked in. "I'm here. Let the party begin!"

"Dr. Bozo," Vince boomed.

"Handy Vinny," Jared shot back with a grin. He was fair like Gabe with dirty blond hair and green eyes, but taller than Gabe and more muscular.

Vince grinned back. "Cut anybody open today?" Jared could've easily been a mechanic, almost as good as Nico with cars and tools, but his biological dad pushed the books with his kids Gabe, Luke, and Jared. Jared did it all too—college, medical school, residency. He was damn proud of him.

"It's Sunday," Jared replied. "We let 'em rest. Who wants a beer? You, you." He pointed around the room at all of them, got a few yeses and headed to the kitchen to fetch them.

"I hope Luke makes it," Gabe said. "I wanted to ask him about college savings accounts." Luke was a Wall Street guy. He specialized in hedge funds, but the family came to him with any and all money questions. He knew it all.

"You're already opening an account?" Vince asked. "He's not even born yet."

"College is expensive," Gabe said. "You've got to start early."

"Then I should start saving while my kid's still a sperm."

"Wouldn't hurt," Gabe said.

They'd just sat down to dinner when Luke joined them. "Sorry I'm late. The bridge traffic was terrible." He lived in New York City. An hour drive with no traffic, but there was always traffic.

Everyone dug in to the food. His dad was the main cook around here, and his food was delicious. Vince waited for a lull in the conversation. Everyone liked to catch up when they got together for Sunday dinner, and their mom asked each of them in turn what was going on in their lives. She picked up right where they'd left off the last time, always remembering what each of them was up to. They'd lucked out getting her for a stepmom.

He still remembered when she'd first joined the family. Vince had been wishing for a mom for three years, every birthday wish, every penny in a fountain, he'd even searched for four-leaf clovers to make a wish on them too. His own mom had been sick for five years with ovarian cancer. He could only remember her as sick, he'd been four when she was diagnosed, nine when she died. They'd had a series of babysitters after she died, but what he wanted more than anything was a mom of his own. The kind he saw on TV, who cooked them dinner and tucked them in at night. When his dad brought Allie home and announced they were getting married, she'd taken the time to sit and talk with each of her new stepsons. It had just been her, not her three boys, which made her feel more like his new mom. She'd been so kind, so pretty, Vince couldn't believe his wish had finally come true. But at twelve, he wasn't about to admit any of his childish dreams.

She'd sat at the kitchen table with him and handed him chocolate chip cookies and a glass of milk. Just like on TV. He'd wolfed down the cookies immediately.

"How do you feel about having a new stepmom?" she'd asked.

"I don't know," he muttered, but on the inside he was excited.

"I could never replace your mom," she said. "I know she was a very special lady."

He stared at the table. "Yeah."

"You can call me Allie if you want," she said. "Or Mom. Whatever you're comfortable with."

He glanced up quickly to find her smiling. Somehow he just knew she'd like being called Mom. And, even though he knew he wasn't honoring his mother like the priest said he should in the ten commandments, the words rolled right off his tongue. "I'll call you Mom."

She beamed, and he knew he'd guessed right. The betrayal of his mom's memory made him squirm, and he looked away. Because for as long as he could remember, he'd wished for a new mom, even when his mom was alive. He couldn't remember a time when she wasn't weak and tired, and he resented not having a mom that could take care of them, like their friends' moms. It was like he'd wished his real mom dead and gone so he could have a better one. Now that his wish had come true, he knew he'd be going to hell. What kind of son does that?

Now there was a lull in the conversation, so Vince plunged in. "Hey, Dad, I've got the papers in the car for the library project. Looks like with some adjustments, the project is ours."

His dad set his fork down. "What kind of adjustments?"

"The town wants to preserve the historic old part, and we're going to rework the design a bit to include brick surround to make it blend."

"You mean the way Capello Construction proposed? That's too expensive."

His brothers watched them back and forth like a tennis match.

"Yeah, about that," Vince said carefully. "They signed off on Capello's design, but named us subcontractor—"

"Subcontractor!" his dad thundered.

"With the majority of crew and work. It's complicated, but Sophia said—"

"Sophia Capello?" A vein pulsed in his dad's forehead.

"Yeah." He cleared his throat. "It seems their company isn't doing too well. They're looking for a partner. Sophia said she could head up a historic architecture department while I run the new construction projects. Of course, I said the library should be a trial project before we moved forward with any kind of—"

"What the hell are you talking about?" His dad's face was red.

"Honey, calm down," his stepmom said. "It's not good for you to be stressed."

"What are you talking about?" his dad said in a calmer voice. "We don't have a historic architecture department. You're running the rest? What is this, a merger? Because I didn't agree to that at all."

Vince held up a hand. "I know it's complicated, but they'd let go of some of their employees, and we'd keep all of ours. We'd knock out our greatest competitor and have the good reputation of both. Not to mention the experienced crew from their side."

"Are you out of your mind?" his dad shouted. So much for not making a scene in front of the family. "What kind of hold does this woman have on you?"

"She's a supermodel," Gabe put in.

"Gabe," Zoe said, shaking her head.

"A matching pair," Nico chimed in, referring to the old joke about Vince's brush with modeling.

"I'll show you a matching pair," Vince growled at Nico, thankful for the interruption for what promised to be a first-class tirade from the head of the family and the business.

"Last time I checked," his dad boomed, "I'm not dead yet. That means I'm still in charge, and it'll be a cold day in hell before I align myself with the likes of Joe Capello."

"He's out of the picture," Vince said. "Sophia's running things, and she needs help. She needs us."

"I'm not giving up everything I worked for so you can hook up with some supermodel!" his dad hollered.

"She's not a damn supermodel!" Vince hollered back. "She's a historic architecture expert!"

"Let's not talk business at the table," his stepmom said in her quiet calm voice. "After dinner."

"Sorry," his dad said, wiping his mouth with a napkin and returning to his meal.

"Sorry, Ma," Vince said.

"So, Zoe, have you and Gabe signed up for baptism class yet?" his mom asked, steering the conversation to neutral ground.

"Yes, we're taking one in November before the baby arrives," Zoe said. "Vince, can you take it too?"

"Sure."

Zoe went on. "And Father Munson says we need to be at church every Sunday if he's going to be baptized there. Godparents too. Okay, Vince?"

Vince hadn't been to church in years, but there was no way he'd let his godson down. "I'll be there."

"Good. My sister, Jasmine, will be there too." Zoe looked around the table. "She's godmother."

"Your sister's little girl is so adorable," his mom said. "It'll be nice for the cousins to grow up together."

Vince calmed down a bit, thinking of his godson. Everyone returned to their meal, teasing each other and talking over each other like usual. Except his dad, who sat there quietly fuming. Vince knew he was going to get an earful once everyone cleared the room. When the meal finished, Vince helped clear the dishes like usual and returned to the dining room to face his dad.

"Let's take a walk," his dad said.

Vince inclined his head and followed his dad out the front door.

"Vince, when I put you in charge of this project, I wasn't handing over the reins completely."

"I can handle it," Vince said. "One day you're going to retire, and you've got me ready and willing to step up. I've earned partner."

"I can't retire if you're going to throw everything I've worked for away on some fling."

Vince took a deep breath. "I'm not. It's more like a partnership. An alliance that could be good for both companies."

"I won't do business with a foulmouthed, bad-tempered stubborn asshole. And that's being nice about it."

Vince couldn't imagine Sophia being so devoted to her dad if he was a complete monster. He suspected pride and stubbornness on both their dads' parts were what kept the hostility level high. "Sophia's not like that."

"You like her," his dad said.

He shrugged. "She's all right."

"Son, there's too much riding on this for you not to be straight with me."

"Nothing's going on."

"Good. The last thing we need is to be connected to *that* family."

Vince kicked some leaves down the sidewalk, quickly deciding to leave the fact that Joe had left the company near bankruptcy out of the conversation. It would come up soon enough if they went forward with a merger. And he'd promised Sophia not to say anything. "Her family's screwed up. She's just caught in the middle."

His dad shook his finger at him. "No alliance. No partnership. Am I making myself clear?"

Vince's stomach dropped. Now he had to come clean. "Dad, Sophia asked for my help, and we worked out a deal."

"What?"

"We worked it out," he repeated. "We'll still get the lion's share of the work. Our name will be right next to theirs at the groundbreaking."

"Dammit, Vince, I thought I could trust you with your first project."

Vince gritted his teeth. "You can. Sophia knows what she's doing on the historic side. It wouldn't hurt us to get more involved with historic projects. A lot of towns around here have a history they want to preserve."

"Listen to you, the freaking history fan. Since when, huh? You sleeping with this woman?"

"No. She's not like that. She's…" Awesome, he finished silently. Feisty, sexy, smart. He stared off in the distance, remembering their last conversation that had gotten a little… spicy. Like Sophia, sweet and spicy. He wanted more of that. It felt unnatural not to go for it. She was just so—

"Ah, shit." His dad shoved a hand in his hair. "Hook up with her on your own time. Don't screw this up, Vince!"

Vince stiffened. "I'm not screwing it up. They're more like consultants. It's mostly our project. This is the only way."

"So who's the boss?"

"I am."

"If I find out she's running things behind the scenes, making a play for our business." His dad shoved both hands in his hair. "This could all be a scam to destroy everything I've worked for."

"She's not like that. She's a straight shooter."

His dad groaned. "This was Joe's plan all along. Send in

his supermodel daughter to turn your head, and then steal the project right out from under us."

"She's not a supermodel. Yes, she's beautiful, but that doesn't mean she's not good for the company. You can't hold that against her."

His dad paced back and forth. "So we're subcontractor or nothing? That's what you're telling me?"

"Yes."

"Dammit. If I find out you're fooling around with this strumpet."

"She's not a strumpet! I don't even know what the hell that is. Don't talk about her."

His dad gave him a look. Vince met his gaze unflinchingly. He'd done nothing wrong, and he'd saved what could have been a loss with the potential for a lot more work for the company.

"I'm not signing a damn thing until I meet her," his dad finally said.

"Why?"

"I want to see what we're up against!"

"She's harmless." He bit back some harsher language he felt like spewing, out of respect for his dad's condition, recovering from chemo. "Just…calm the frick down."

"Tomorrow night. Bring her by the house. Either she shows or she goes."

"Fine!" he barked.

9

─────────

Sophia had just settled on the sofa with a glass of red wine and a book when the doorbell rang. She peeked through the peephole. Vince! She smoothed her hair and tied the belt on her red silk robe a little tighter.

She opened the door, and he barged in. "It's not going to work," he said. His hair was wet like he'd just taken a shower. His woodsy, masculine scent filled the space, making her almost woozy with lust.

"What are you doing here?" she asked. "It's late."

"I just came from working out, and I looked at it from every angle—" He stopped and took her in from head to toe. "Whadda ya got on underneath that robe?"

"I wasn't expecting anyone. I'll change." Before she could take one step, he snagged the arm holding the book.

"Whatcha reading?" he asked in a teasing tone.

She hid the book behind her back. "Nothing. What do you mean it won't work out?"

"*The Mistress and The Rake*? Do you want to be a mistress?" He barked out a laugh. "Are you looking for a rake? Is that like a player?"

She stiffened. "My friend left it here. I normally only read, um…"

"Shakespeare?"

"Yes! Shakespeare and-and Tolstoy."

"Any good sex scenes in there? I read a doozy of one in my ex-girlfriend's stash."

"I just skip over those scenes." She looked away from those gleaming, knowing eyes. "Kinda boring actually."

"Uh-huh."

She crossed her arms. "Why are you here again?"

He snagged the book out of her hands and read out loud. "'Why, Maurice, you can't mean to bed me here?' she asked in a breathy voice." He grinned. "Let's hear your breathy voice."

"I don't have one."

He stepped into her personal space and brushed her hair back over her ear, and then that devious rake leaned in close enough to make his voice rumble in her ear. "I bet you do."

"I don't," she breathed.

He kept rumbling in her ear. "Say 'you can't mean to bed me here.'"

She jerked away. "Like hell."

He grinned. "I love messing with you."

She turned on her heel and flopped down on the sofa. She caught him staring and looked down to see the front of her robe had opened. Geez. She refastened it so she was covered decently and grabbed the lap blanket she kept on the sofa. He sat next to her and pulled the blanket so it went across both their laps. Most of it was on him. Was he covering a hard-on? She flushed, uncomfortably aware of the skimpiness of her thin robe and panties next to this sexy lumberjack she was unaccountably drawn to. He was extremely aggravating.

And she'd enjoyed the butt rub he'd given her a little too much.

"This is cozy," he said.

"I'm losing patience with you," she said.

"What happens when you run out?" he asked.

She gritted her teeth. "Just tell me why you're here." The tension was unbearable. Was he going to make a move or not? She'd been imagining those rough calloused hands on her more than was reasonable for a busy woman with a lot of other important things she should be focused on. Of course, having lusty thoughts was very different from actually carrying through on them. She casually shifted away from the heat of that large, thick, muscular body.

He let out a long breath. "Yeah. My dad is not going for the partnership idea. He was pretty irate about it. Has a big thing against your dad, as you know."

"Oh."

"So…I dunno. I think we're back to square one. He's the boss."

She shifted to face him. "Well, so is my dad, but who's really running things on the ground day to day? You and me. That's who!"

He held up a hand. "Preaching to the choir."

"What about this? The library project we work just like we agreed, shared resources, me in charge of the historic end as a trial. If it goes well, then they'll have to agree the merger idea could work."

Vince ran a hand through his hair. "Yeah. Well, I'm okay with that, but my dad…"

"How close is he to retirement?"

"I don't know. He was rumbling about it before, but now he's pulling rank. What about your dad?"

She thought about that. "I don't know if I'd say he wants to retire so much as he doesn't want to do anything anymore. That's how I ended up here."

"Did you run the partnership idea by him?"

She looked straight ahead and admitted, "I was waiting to see how it went on your end first."

"So you just let me take the heat?"

She glanced over, expecting him to be really angry, but he was looking at her more like he was fascinated with whatever she was about to say. She lifted one shoulder up and down. "I figured why get into it with my dad if it was a no-go with yours."

"You figured, huh?"

"Yes."

He tickled her, and she shrieked in surprise. Then she tickled him back, connected with a hard stomach, and he grabbed her hands and wrapped them around his waist, making her hug him. She looked up at him, puzzled.

"Hey, you feel like coming to dinner at my parents' house tomorrow night?" he asked, not even bothering to look at her.

Her jaw dropped. "You want me to meet your parents?"

He let out a long sigh. Still not looking at her. "Yes."

"Really?"

"Really."

"Okay. Should I bring anything?"

He released her hands, straightened, and finally looked at her. "Just yourself. Wear a dress."

"Is it formal?"

"No."

"Then why the dress?"

"For me."

Her brows shot up. "Are you playing with me?"

"I'm not playing." He rubbed the back of his neck. "For once I'm not playing."

"I'm not dressing to please you."

"Fine. Wear what you want. It's casual."

"You sound like you don't really want me there."

"No, no, I do." He stared at the floor, frowning. In that moment, she knew what the invitation was about. She was being summoned by the senior Marino. He wanted to meet her before moving forward with anything. Still, it was a good sign. Better than a flat refusal. It was clear Vince's hands were tied, and he wasn't happy about not being able to sign off on the contract and move forward like she did. Her dad had given her the authority to run the business, putting her name on everything important just before he'd retreated to his hidey-hole. For some reason, Vince didn't have the authority to sign off on this project, even though he'd represented the company for it.

"Are you going to feel me up after?" she teased to cheer him up.

He flashed a smile that lit up his face. "Do you want me to feel you up after?"

She smacked his arm. "Of course not, you rake!"

He laughed. "I'm getting a copy of that book."

"Look out, ladies. Vince is getting an instruction manual."

"I don't need an instruction manual. I know where everything is." He raised his brows. "Trust me."

"I'll have to take your word on that."

"Sophia," he said quietly.

"What?"

His gaze was warm and direct. "Thank you."

"You're welcome."

He stood. "Enjoy your rake." And then he left just as suddenly as he'd arrived.

She sat there for a moment, musing over the man she was beginning to suspect had a tender center hidden under all that hard muscle and macho bravado, and then she returned to her book. Only this time she kept imagining Vince as the rake.

Sophia sat across from Vince at his parents' dining room table, trying to appear relaxed. His dad had been polite, but she felt the tension rolling off him and knew it was just a matter of time before he got to whatever point he wanted to make.

"Can we eat?" Vince asked, rolling his neck. Bread and salad were on the table, but the main course was warming on the stove. His mom had made Italian wedding soup for the health benefits she said, but Sophia was suspicious about some misplaced matchmaking intentions between her and Vince, especially when Mr. Marino had scowled at that comment.

"Nico will be here," Mrs. Marino said.

Vince drummed his fingers on the table. "Why?"

"Does your brother need a reason to come home for dinner?" his dad asked.

"Angel too," his mom said.

Vince stared at his dad. "Again, why?"

"Because we're talking Marino family business," his dad said evenly.

"But they don't want to be in construction," Vince said.

Sophia tensed. Was Mr. Marino handing over the business to his three sons? Was she about to watch an all-out war between Vince and the rest of the Marino clan?

A man appeared, grinning a dimpled smile at them. "I'm here."

Vince jerked his chin. "Angel."

"Sophia, this is Vince's youngest brother Angelo," his mom said. He was about her height, five ten or so, lean and lithe, unlike Vince's massive bulk. His hair was dark brown and rumpled adorably.

Angel shook her hand. "Nice to meet you."

"You too."

He sat next to her and looked around the table. "What're we having?"

"Italian wedding soup," their mom said.

Angel's brows shot up. "Really?"

"Switch seats with me, Angel." Vince got up and stood next to his brother, waiting. Angel switched without question. Vince dropped into the seat next to her, which put him between her and his dad.

"How're you feeling, Dad?" Angel asked once he was settled again.

"Fine, fine," Mr. Marino said.

"Do we need Gabe, Luke, and Jared to weigh in on Marino construction too?" Vince asked.

"Just the original three," Mr. Marino said.

Vince grunted and turned to her. "How're you doing?"

"I'm fine," she said. As if she always sat at tense family dinners waiting for the other shoe to drop.

"You want some wine?" he asked.

"Sure," she said.

Vince left the table. Sophia smiled tightly, darting a quick glance around the table. She could feel Mr. Marino studying her.

"You don't look much like your father," Mr. Marino said.

She nodded. "I took after my mother." Vince, on the other hand, looked a lot like his dad.

Vince returned, handing her a glass of red wine. "Thank you."

"What exactly do you do, Sophia?" Mr. Marino asked.

"Dad, don't give her the third degree," Vince said.

"It's not the third degree," Mr. Marino said. "It's a simple question."

"I work for a consulting firm that helps preserve historic homes and buildings," Sophia said.

"I see," Mr. Marino said.

"Business after dinner," Vince said, shooting his dad a hard look.

His dad grunted, grabbed a piece of bread and took a big bite.

"I'm here, I'm here, you can eat!" a beautiful man announced. It must be Nico. He had the same dark good looks as Vince, but not as large in build. Tall and muscular all the same. He looked right at her, flashed a brilliant smile, and her breath caught. He had movie-star good looks.

"Hello," Nico said warmly to her.

"No," Vince said.

"Hi," she said.

Nico kissed Mrs. Marino's cheek and took the seat on the other side of Sophia. "I'm Nico." He shook her hand in a firm, warm grip.

"I'm Sophia."

"What a beautiful name," Nico said, still holding her hand. "So-phi-a."

Vince reached over and smacked Nico upside the head. "Ow!" He dropped her hand and rubbed his head.

"Vince!" Sophia said.

"I knew it!" Mr. Marino said, pounding his fist on the table. "He couldn't keep it in his pants."

"It's in my pants!" Vince exclaimed.

"Vincent Marino, not at the table," Mrs. Marino said, glaring at both the senior and junior Vincents. She stood. "I'll get the soup. Sophia, would you like to help?"

She got up. "I'd love to."

She followed Mrs. Marino into the kitchen and waited

while she ladled the soup into thick white bowls. "I thought maybe you'd like a break from the testosterone poisoning in there," Mrs. Marino said. "You seem like a nice, sane woman."

Sophia laughed. "Thank you."

"Could you grab the tray?" She indicated a large tray on the opposite counter. Sophia brought it over. "So are you and Vince a couple?"

Sophia felt herself flush. "No, we just work together. I guess his dad wanted to meet me because of the library project."

"Hmmm..." She set a bowl of soup on the tray. Sophia helped her arrange the bowls. "Did you know Vince was a star football player in high school? Wide receiver."

Sophia shook her head. "I didn't know that." But it wasn't a huge surprise, he'd mentioned playing football, she just hadn't known he was the star player. Of course, given his size...and all that glorious muscle. *Get a grip.*

Mrs. Marino finished putting the bowls on the tray and lifted it, inclining her head for Sophia to follow her into the dining room. "He's a little more...spirited than the others, but if you channel that right—"

"Ma, are you talking about me?" Vince boomed.

Sophia grinned, and Vince shot her a dark look.

Mrs. Marino set the tray on the table and gave Vince an exasperated look. "Lower your volume."

Nico and Angel laughed. Mr. Marino remained serious.

Sophia took her seat next to Vince and leaned close. "I heard you were a star football player."

Vince made a face. "Ma, no one cares what I did in high school."

"Did you know Vince could've been a model?" Nico asked.

Vince scowled. "Shut it."

Sophia grinned at Vince. "I'm learning all sorts of things about you tonight." She looked around the table. "What else you got on him? Gimme the dirt."

Vince jabbed his finger at his brothers each in turn, a silent warning. "Let's eat."

Everyone started eating, and Sophia figured the teasing had stopped.

"Vince taught me how to defend myself," Angel said. "It came in handy, especially in middle school. I don't know if I ever thanked you for that. Thanks, Vince."

Vince waved that away. "He was a shrimp. Someone had to help him out. Jared looked out for you too."

Sophia looked at Vince, seeing him in a whole new light. One who cared deeply about his family. She should've known when he showed her the ultrasound of his godson that first time they'd had dinner, but she'd been distracted by his aggressive player persona. A surge of affection ran through her. She kinda wanted to hug him. *Aargh.* She was toast—burned by proximity to the fiery way-too-sexy Italian lumberjack.

"The soup is really good," Sophia told Mrs. Marino.

Mrs. Marino beamed. "It's Mr. Marino's recipe. He's the genius chef around here."

"Oh, now, Allie," Mr. Marino said affectionately, looking cheerful for the first time all night. Clearly Sophia was putting a damper on his evening. She hoped she could smooth things over for her dad and work something out with Vince's dad. "You're becoming a genius chef in your own right."

"You know who can make a great steak?" Nico asked, jerking a thumb in Vince's direction.

Vince groaned.

Angel chimed in. "One time I dropped my double-scoop ice cream cone and Vince gave me his."

"They're really singing your praises tonight," Sophia said with a smile.

"And they can stop," Vince said. "Nothing's going on with me and Sophia; nothing's going to go on no matter how many Vince stories you tell her. It's a professional relationship. End of story."

Sophia stared at her soup, surprisingly disappointed.

Vince couldn't have given her a clearer message than that. He'd just been playing around with her before with the flirting and teasing and...butt rub. He probably acted like that with every woman he met. She was nothing special. She'd wasted too much time fantasizing about those large hands and that body. She straightened and gave herself a mental slap. The business was all that mattered, not her inappropriate lustful feelings. Not her misplaced affection.

"Eat more soup, Vince," Mrs. Marino said. "You too, Sophia."

Sophia complied. It was really good. Growing up, she'd had to teach herself to cook because her dad was always busy with work and her mom was more interested in her social life than her children. It was either that or live off crackers. And she had her younger brother to look out for too.

"Face it, Vince," Nico said. "You need all the help you can get."

"Butt out," Vince said.

"You don't get this kind of girl ever," Nico said, looking right at Sophia. "She's a classy lady."

Sophia was about to thank Nico for the compliment when Vince leaned across Sophia and grabbed Nico by the collar. "You're going to be kissing this table in a minute."

"He needs taming, Sophia," Nico said with a big smile, not seeming at all worried about kissing the table. "Save us all."

She flushed. She wasn't sure what to say. She had no influence over Vince whatsoever, but it seemed his family thought differently.

Vince dropped his brother's shirt, stared at his plate for a minute, and then shook his head. "Sorry my family is so embarrassing, Sophia. I had no idea they were going to try to convince you of my virtues."

"Did you know Vince can ballroom dance?" Mrs. Marino asked.

Vince groaned and looked to the ceiling. Sophia couldn't help but laugh.

"We all can," Angel put in. "We had lessons."

"I'm done with you all." Vince went back to eating.

Sophia grinned. "How did that happen?"

Mrs. Marino told the story about how she sent the boys, along with Mr. Marino, to dance lessons before their wedding. Mr. Marino filled in some of the blanks about the boys' antics in the dance studio while everyone laughed and talked over each other. Even Vince joined in. For a short time, Sophia felt like she belonged to a real family.

Vince cleared the table, more embarrassed than he'd ever been in his life. He couldn't believe the way his family went on and on about him. Like Sophia cared about double-scoop ice cream cones and high school football. He'd never brought a woman home before, and tonight just proved why that had been a smart move.

"Let's walk, son," his dad said, pulling a jacket on. "You too, Sophia."

"Sure," she said.

Vince helped her into her jacket. The minute they hit the sidewalk, his dad started the questions.

"Sophia, what exactly do you have in mind for Capello Construction, and why do you need us?"

"Well, as you might've heard, Capello has been struggling for a bit. I thought our two companies working together could help both of us stay competitive."

"We're already competitive," his dad said. "The way I see it, you need us. We don't need you."

"Sophia has ideas for a historic architecture department," Vince put in. "A whole new market we could reach. And we could get into residential construction too."

"We don't need that," his dad said. "Commercial sector is plenty."

"It reduces competition for bids if Capello and Marino aren't always trying to underbid each other," Sophia said. "It would keep the bid high. And I already have a very wealthy donor lined up to help with the library fundraising, so it's looking better than ever that they can reach their goal and release the municipal bond."

Vince turned, surprised. "You do?"

She nodded. "He's a friend."

Vince narrowed his eyes. "Who?"

"He wants to remain anonymous."

His dad stopped on the sidewalk. "Sophia, your dad and I have a history. Not a good one."

Sophia cringed. "I know."

"It didn't have to be that way," his dad said. "We used to be best friends."

"What!" Vince exclaimed. "You never told me that. I thought you always hated him."

"We played football together," his dad said. "We were close. Until Maria." Vince jerked at the mention of his mother. "She picked me. Joe was so angry. He did everything he could to sabotage me. Slashed my tires when I took her out. Stole my football jersey before the game. He was unstoppable. That man can hold a grudge."

Vince knew all that. Sophia looked shocked. Guess she'd heard a different version of things.

"I'm so sorry," Sophia said.

"He underbid every project I went after," his dad informed Sophia. "He stole so much business from us. He couldn't stand that Maria and I were so happy. Guess he got the last laugh. She died young. I was devastated."

"I'm sure he wasn't laughing," Sophia said. "I'm so sorry for your loss."

His dad shook his head. "Let's just say I know what kind of man he is. Not the kind I would ever do business with. How could I trust him?"

"You can trust me," Sophia said. "I'll retain control of the library project. It's an area he knows nothing about."

Vince looked to his dad, who seemed to be thinking it over.

"You got any skeletons in your closet?" his dad asked. "Tell me about you."

"What would you like to know?" Sophia asked.

"Who you spend time with, what your parents were like growing up, where do you see yourself in five years."

"Oh." Sophia glanced at Vince. "That covers quite a lot."

"Dad, be serious."

His dad held a hand up to shush him.

They resumed walking. "Start at the beginning," his dad said.

10

<hr>

Sophia began to talk, and Vince listened as her answers revealed a very different side to the sophisticated woman he'd been sparring with these last two weeks. "I have friends in Brooklyn I spend time with," she said. "Growing up, I spent a lot of time at my friend Laura's house. Her mom was always there after school, ready to feed us a snack and ask us about our day."

"Where was your mom?" his dad asked.

Sophia waved her hand. "In and out. She had a very busy social life. My little brother, Mike, went to a babysitter after school, but my parents let me go to Laura's. Mike's five years younger."

"And your dad?" his dad asked.

"Busy. Very busy. I'd see him on the weekends. He'd give me gifts and then head out with my mom. They were very close."

But what she didn't say was that they were very close to her or her brother. In fact, she sounded like she was on her own a lot.

"My brother was very busy with sports," Sophia said. "I didn't have a thing, you know? I mean, eventually I discovered art and history and architecture, but they don't have much of that for kids. It was fine. I had Laura and I was close to one of my teachers."

Holy shit. That was it? One friend and a teacher. She sounded practically like an orphan.

"Your dad ever mention me?" his dad asked.

"Only when he was mad," she said. "He thought you had it out for him."

"He had it out for me."

"I know there are two sides to every story," Sophia said diplomatically, which Vince thought was awfully big of her. He wasn't so quick to forgive a slight against his family.

"Where do you see yourself in five years?" his dad asked.

"Dad, you sound like you're interviewing her."

"Maybe I am."

"I hope to still be doing what I'm doing," Sophia answered. "Working on interesting historic projects."

His dad grunted. "Vince, did you bring the library plans like I asked?"

"Yes."

"Let's go look them over."

They went back to the house. Vince laid out the blueprints on the dining room table, which had been cleared while they were out. His dad turned to Sophia. "Tell me what you see here. Tell me about the history too."

Sophia launched into a long explanation on the history of the library and how the new section would complement the old and bring so much to the town. Her passion for history and architecture came through loud and clear. And she knew a helluva lot more about construction than he'd realized. He thought maybe his dad was surprised too because he raised a brow at Vince over Sophia's head. Vince shrugged.

"Thanks for answering an old man's questions," his dad said to Sophia. "Could you give Vince and me a moment alone? Get yourself some dessert if you want."

Sophia nodded and headed for the kitchen. Vince followed his dad to the living room, where Nico and Angel were sprawled on the sofa, feet up on the coffee table, watching the Red Sox game. Vince wished he could join them.

His dad checked the score, picked up the remote, and muted the game.

"Vince, take a seat," his dad said.

Angel scooted over, and Vince sat next to him. Three Marino brothers sitting at attention on the sofa waiting for the proclamation from the boss. Why were his brothers here? Vince tamped down his irritation. Now that he knew the history with his dad and Joe Capello, how they had once been close, he was more determined than ever to end this nonsense between them. They didn't have to be friends, just stop being enemies long enough for their businesses to do better.

"What's up, Dad?" Vince asked. He hoped this wasn't related to the cancer. He'd thought they wouldn't hear any news until his three-month checkup.

His dad stepped closer and lowered his voice. "Nico, what'd you think of Sophia?"

Nico lifted one shoulder up and down. "I liked her. Too good for Vince over here." Vince leaned over Angel to give Nico a shove. "But she's cool."

"Angel?" his dad asked.

"I think she's a good person. Direct and honest. What did you think of her?" Angel often turned questions around because of his social worker training. So annoying.

"Dad, why're you asking them about Sophia?" Vince asked in as quiet a voice as he could muster. He didn't want Sophia to know they were talking about her. "This doesn't concern them."

"If I'm going to consider partnering with Capello Construction on this project—" his dad made a face "—it does concern them. When I go, my assets go to the three of you, including the business. Gabe, Luke, and Jared wanted it that way. They already inherited a good amount of money from their biological father."

"I thought I was taking over Marino and Sons?" Vince barked. "You're talking about selling it off as an asset?"

His dad put a hand up. "Calm down. You can still be partner, but your brothers also get the chance to join the business."

"They don't want that!" Vince couldn't believe this. He was the one who put in sixteen years of hard labor in the business. Not his brothers.

"Dad, that's a nice offer, but I wouldn't know the first thing about construction," Angel said. "This is Vince's deal."

"I got my own shop," Nico said. "I like it that way." Nico owned Exotic and Classic Restorations, where he restored and sold some really cool cars. It was where Vince got his Camaro.

His dad grunted. "I just wanted to put it out there. I, uh, I'm working on my will with Gabe's help. I just want to make sure you're all taken care of."

"What did the doctors say?" Vince asked.

"No news," his dad said. "Not until my checkup. I just thought it was a smart thing to do. I'm getting up there in age."

"You're sixty!" Vince said. "Not that old."

"Just to be on the safe side," his dad said somberly. Vince knew exactly why. This cancer diagnosis had shaken them all up.

"I'm comfortable with Vince taking over the family business," Angel said. "I don't need any assets. Vince, you keep it going as long as you like. You don't have to check in with me."

"Thank you." He put Angel in a headlock and rubbed the top of his head. Angel grinned. "I knew I kept you around for a reason."

"Yeah, I'm out." Nico grabbed the remote. "It's all you, Vince. Can we watch the game?"

His dad frowned. "Here I thought my legacy meant something to you boys."

"It means something to me, Dad," Vince said. Once again he felt passed over. He wasn't good enough to trust with the family business.

His dad crossed his arms and studied Vince for a long moment. "All right. Let's see how this library project goes with you and Sophia running it. As long as her dad's not involved. But—" he held up a finger "—there will be no merger as long as Joe's at the head of the company."

"That's fair," Vince said.

His dad rubbed the back of his neck. "Don't do anything stupid, Vince."

Vince's head reared back. "Like what?"

"Like getting involved with the person you're supposed to be working with. I need to know this isn't some harebrained scheme just to seduce a beautiful woman."

Vince stood, beyond annoyed. "You met her, you saw the plans, had your interrogation; I'm taking her home now."

"This is your proving ground," his dad said. "Show me what you can do."

He'd spent his whole life proving himself. He'd thought sixteen years of working for the old man had shown what he could do. Obviously that wasn't enough.

He found Sophia sitting at the dining room table with a cup of tea, chatting with his stepmom. "Let's go, Sophia."

Her eyes widened. "But we haven't had dessert yet. Your mom made these almond crescent cookies. I had one. They're so good."

Vince glanced at the plate of cookies covered in powdered sugar and immediately became suspicious. First the Italian wedding soup and now the cookies his stepmom always made for weddings with his Italian relatives.

"Are you trying to tell me something, Ma?" he asked.

She sipped her tea. "I have no idea what you're referring to."

There was no way he was going to bring it up in front of Sophia. He didn't want her getting any ideas that he was looking for marriage. Why would his stepmom think that just because he brought a woman home for the first time he was looking for a wife? He'd only invited her because his dad insisted.

His stepmom held the tray out to him. "Have a cookie."

"Did someone say cookies?" Angel asked. He got a napkin and grabbed a handful. "Nico," he called, "you want cookies?"

Nico appeared and snagged a handful. "Love when you bake, Ma."

"It's my pleasure," his stepmom said. She picked up a cookie and held it out to Vince. Suddenly that cookie felt like an invitation to a domestic ball and chain, and he was not prepared to go there.

"No, thanks," he managed.

"Come on, just one," she coaxed. "Sophia had one."

Sophia nodded and smiled.

"I'm on a diet," he said, which made his brothers laugh uproariously. Angel started choking, and Nico pounded him on the back. "It's late. We gotta go." He leaned down and kissed his stepmom's cheek. "Thanks for dinner."

His stepmom pressed the cookie in his hand with a sweet smile. "For the road."

He hung his head. Now what was he supposed to do with the damn thing?

"Eat it, eat it," Nico chanted.

"He's got to watch his figure," Angel said before cracking up again.

Sophia stood, looking amused. "I'll take it if you don't want it."

He shoved it in his mouth. "Happy?"

His stepmom hid a smile. His dad walked in and snagged a cookie.

"Thank you for your hospitality," Sophia said to his parents. She turned to his brothers. "It was nice meeting you both."

"You too," they chorused.

His dad shook her hand. "I'm glad to see you're your own person."

"Thank you," Sophia said, all graciousness and class even with the not-so-subtle dig at her father. "Nice to meet you too."

They said their goodbyes. His stepmom threw in one last-ditch effort on Vince's behalf. Sort of. "Remember what I said, Sophia. Don't let him walk all over you. He respects strength."

"Ma, I'm right here," Vince moaned.

Sophia laughed. "No danger of that."

"Good. I hope we'll see you again."

Sophia smiled and nodded. He doubted she'd ever want to face his family again. Not after all the embarrassing comments and the hard questions his dad had asked her. Hadn't exactly been a picnic. He walked her out the door and into his car. When she got in, she leaned her head back on the seat and blew out a breath, closing her eyes.

"Sorry about that," he said.

"That was rough with your dad," she said.

"You did all right." His gaze lingered on her. Her eyes were still closed, her long lashes fanning out over those smooth cheeks. She looked sweet almost, with her eyes closed. Her spicy rose scent drew him in. She opened her eyes and returned his stare. A jolt of desire gripped him. Her eyes held such fire. He was so tempted just to—

"You going to stare at me all day, or are you going to start the car?" she asked.

He grinned and started the car. "You did good, Soph. Real good. Thank you."

"You think your dad will let us partner on the library?"

He pulled out into the street. "He said so when we spoke."

"I passed the test!" She raised a fist in the air. "Woo-hoo!"

He laughed. "Yeah, you passed. But he only wants you on the job. Not your dad."

"No problem." She was quiet for a moment. "You have a nice family."

"They're all right."

"You're a good big brother. A good son."

He warmed at the compliment. No one ever used the word "good" about him, though tonight his family had been full of praise. All for Sophia's benefit, but still. "Eh, you're just saying that because Ma gave you an earful tonight. No one told you the bad stuff."

"What bad stuff?"

He got quiet. He didn't tell anyone that shit.

"Let me guess," she said, "you're some kind of man whore?"

He grinned. "That would imply I get paid."

"Man slut?"

"I enjoy women. That's all. I'm upfront that I'm not looking for anything serious." Unfortunately, his stepmom had other ideas with all that wedding food. "Everyone knows going in what they're gonna get. Nobody gets hurt."

"How do you know?"

He stopped at a stop sign and looked over at her. "How do I know what?"

"How do you know nobody gets hurt? Do you talk to them about it later? Make sure they're okay?"

"Pfft. No. I don't call them at all. They call me if they want a repeat performance." He tapped the steering wheel and hit the accelerator. "I tell them that upfront too."

"Classy."

"Thank you."

"I will never be one of those women."

He feigned shock. "No! Really?" She scowled, and he tried really hard not to smile because he could tell she'd been thinking about being his. "I never thought you would be," he added for good measure.

Lie. He'd thought about it way too much. Why shouldn't he give in to a very natural attraction? Just because of the business. His dad's words came back to him, *Don't do anything stupid, Vince.* His dad expected him to screw up even after all the hard work he'd put in. If that was what he expected anyway, why shouldn't he have a little fun? His dad wouldn't have to know. He could keep business and pleasure separate. Probably. It was uncharted territory, and the idea of having Sophia was turning him on way too much for any further rational thinking.

"Good," Sophia said. "I'm glad." But he could tell she wasn't glad at all. She sounded miffed. Maybe she wanted this just as much as he did. He decided to test the waters.

"So tell me more about this fictional rake you get off on," Vince said, glancing over at her.

She straightened. "I don't get off on rakes."

"What gets you off?"

She got mad. He could tell by the way she took a few deep

breaths, and now her lips were practically a flat line. He suppressed a laugh that he knew would just piss her off.

"I am not having this conversation with you," she bit out.

It occurred to him that maybe she didn't get off at all, which was concerning. A beautiful healthy woman like Sophia never experiencing ecstasy.

"Did your last boyfriend get you off?" he asked.

"This is an extremely inappropriate conversation from someone who only wants a—" she made finger quotes in the air "—'professional relationship. End of story.'"

He recognized his own words from dinner as well as the tension in her that he knew he could help out with. "I was just trying to get my family to shut up with the Vince stories." He lowered his voice to a husky drawl. "So, tell me, did your last boyfriend get you off?"

She squirmed a bit, blushing, and finally said, "You mean Simon?" Like he knew all about her ex-boyfriends.

"Yeah," he said just so she'd keep talking.

"Not really." She said it with such sadness that it really started to bug him. Someone like Sophia never feeling passion. It couldn't be. She was full of fire. It wasn't healthy not to get that out.

"What about the guy before that?" he asked.

"Brian?" she asked. Even their names sounded pansy-ass.

"Yeah."

She hesitated. "Almost."

"Almost?" He let out a huge breath of exasperation. What was wrong with these guys? What was wrong with Sophia that she'd settle for less? "Guy before that."

"Tim?" Another pansy-ass name. He was sensing a pattern here.

"Yeah, Tim."

"Not really."

"The rich donor guy?" he asked. "The *friend*."

"He, uh, plays for the other team now." She waved a hand in the air. "So, you know, no."

He bit back a groan. "Sophia."

"I know, but he said he was confused for a while. It wasn't me."

He pulled over to the side of the road somewhere in Clover Park. "Has any guy ever gotten you off? I'm talking fingers fisting in the sheets, raw, screaming-top-of-your-lungs orgasm?"

She flushed, but she still answered. "No."

He stared at her. She stared back, a defiant gleam in her eyes, an unquestionable challenge.

"You want me to show you?" he asked. *Please let me show you.* He knew they'd be good together, and he wanted to be the one, *the first* to witness her ecstasy.

She turned away. "Like you could," she mumbled under her breath.

He caught her chin and turned her back to him. "I promise you I can. One night."

"I don't do one-night stands."

"Two nights," he amended, feeling generous. It was the least he could do. It wouldn't be fair to show her the peak only to drop her back to the low boring side so quickly.

"If you could hear yourself right now, you wouldn't be smirking like that."

"I'm not smirking," he said. "I'm smiling."

"Just take me home, Vince. I'm exhausted."

He pulled back into the street. "Your loss."

She snorted. "Whatever."

Damn, he'd really been hoping.

"It wouldn't affect our business deal," he said, in case that was what was holding her back. He decided then and there, it wouldn't hold him back. "We'll keep that separate. What happens in the bedroom, stays in the bedroom. No one has to know."

Truth was, he had nothing to lose. His dad already thought he was a screwup. That was made abundantly clear to him tonight. And the more time he spent with Sophia, the sharper the hunger for her grew. And, strangely, the more he got to know her, the more he wanted to know. She was addicting. He glanced at her. She appeared to be thinking it over.

"You ever been in love?" she finally asked. "I mean really in love, heart-thumping, head-over-heels, can't-even-think-straight love."

"Nope. Not once."

"You don't sound torn up about it."

"I'm not. What about you?"

"No," she said, sounding very forlorn. "I've sort of given up."

"Well, geez, don't give up if that's what you want. What are you, twenty-five?"

"Twenty-six."

"You're young. I'm sure some pansy-ass guy is just waiting around the corner for you, dying to profess his love."

She brightened. "Yeah? You really think so?"

"Sure."

"One of the town council members has a son he wants to set me up with."

"Who?"

"You know Randy? His son."

"Out of the question," Vince said.

"Why? He said he's in pharmaceutical sales. Stable, good job, looking to settle down."

"First of all, Randy is a lech."

"He is not."

"Trust me," Vince said, "I know. Second of all, a sales guy is not going to get you off. You can do better than that." Like me.

"Who should I date? Huh? A guy like you? No, thanks."

"What's wrong with me?"

"Two nights!" She gestured wildly. "That's a fucking proposition, not a date!"

His lips twitched. Something about the f-word coming out of her classy mouth gave him hope. Now that she was looking at yet another pansy-ass boyfriend, he wanted a chance to throw his own name in the ring. Nothing pansy-ass about him. And though he'd never actually dated, more like one-and-done hookups, he suddenly really wanted a date.

"You want to go on a date with me, Soph?"

"It would've been nice to be asked."

He double-checked to see if she was serious. Her arms were crossed, and she was staring mulishly out the front window. "Fine. You want to go to dinner with me?"

"Where to?"

"I don't know. Wherever."

"No."

"Why not?"

"Because I don't think you really want to go. You're just saying that because I got mad."

He felt like pulling his hair out. This woman made no sense. He'd switched gears from a roll in the hay to a classy date like he thought she wanted, and she still didn't go for it. What exactly did she want? He put the radio on and didn't say another word until he pulled up to her house. He studied her. She looked tense. Must be all that pent-up fire with no place to go.

He pushed a lock of hair over her ear. It was silky smooth. He leaned closer. "I'm getting mixed signals here. You into me or what?"

"Or what," she replied. She got out of the car and slammed the door.

Guess he had his answer. Still, he couldn't help watching her hips sway as she marched up the front sidewalk. No way in hell she was going out with that lech Randy's son. For the first time in his life, he worried if he could ever be the kind of man someone might actually want to be with more than once.

He had a feeling one night with Sophia wouldn't be enough.

11

———

A week later, late Friday afternoon, Vince returned to the office to find a FedEx package with the signed contract for the Clover Park Library. His dad had finally signed off on it. He called Sophia's work number and actually got her.

"Hey, Vince, what's up?"

"My dad signed the papers, so full steam ahead."

"That's great! I sent the plans over to my architect. I wanted to see if she could add more windows."

"And?"

"She said she could."

"Send me the plans."

"I will. I'm starting the historic documentation next week."

Vince was surprised to find he had no complaints so far about working with Sophia. She was efficient and professional.

"So let's talk money," he said. "Where are we with the fundraising? How soon before we can break ground?"

"I have a meeting with the fundraising committee next week. We've reached seventy percent of the goal."

"That's with your private donor?"

"Yes. He contributed two million."

Vince whistled under his breath. "Can we break ground

before hitting one hundred percent? I'd really like to get started. We both could use the cash flow."

"I meet with the mayor and town council next week."

"And you forgot to invite me to this meeting?" he asked tightly. "Nice to go behind my back."

"I just needed to get the job done," she replied calmly. "Project's moving forward. That's what you wanted, isn't it?"

"I thought we were partners." It was like she didn't trust him to do the job. "And who the hell is this private donor?"

"We *are* partners."

"Well, it doesn't feel that way. It feels like you're running around setting up meetings and schmoozing donors without me."

"My friend wants to remain anonymous," she said.

Vince didn't like being in the dark. It meant he wasn't trusted.

She went on. "I'm hoping we can get started in six weeks. Thirty of my best guys will show up and work under your direction."

He rocked back on his heels. "And what will you do?"

"Consult on the historic preservation side like we said."

Vince planted his feet firmly on the ground. "Who's the boss?"

"What do you mean?"

"I mean when a decision has to be made about the project, who makes it?"

"We both do."

"Wrong. I do."

"Vince, I thought we were working together."

"Yes, under my leadership."

"That hardly seems fair."

He sensed a win and relaxed considerably. "You need me."

"That doesn't mean—"

"We sealed the deal," he reminded her.

She let out a heavy sigh. "I told you a butt rub didn't count."

He bit back a smile. "What counts?"

"Now you're just teasing."

"I want to see you." The words were out before he realized it was what he really wanted.

"Why?"

"I just do."

"When?"

"Tonight."

"Where?"

He hadn't thought that far ahead. "What do you like to do?" He hoped it didn't require too much exertion. He'd been working hard all week on that shopping center roof.

"You want to meet for drinks?" she asked.

"You like wings?"

"Who doesn't?"

"Drinks and wings at Garner's. It's in Clover Park. I'll swing by to pick you up at seven. Gimme your cell number in case I'm running late."

She rattled off the number.

"Got it." He hung up.

Sophia hung up and considered what she'd just agreed to. Did Vince want more than just a working relationship? Did she? She was unfocused and jittery the rest of the day. Finally, she headed home, changed out of her work clothes and into jeans with a sheer gauzy shirt over a camisole. Vince showed up on time, freshly showered and smelling delicious.

He held the door of the car open for her. When she got in, he said, "Did you tell your dad we're working together?"

"No. He won't notice."

"Isn't he going to notice you've got some of my guys on payroll?"

"Only if he looks over the books. He hasn't been in the office in more than a month."

"He's going to disown you."

"He needs me too much. Besides, I'm selling the house in

Greenport so he can make the company whole again. He'll be grateful to be off the hook."

Vince raised a brow. "Does he know you're selling the house?"

"I'll tell him when we get a viable offer."

He shook his head. "You're devious."

"Resourceful."

"Hmmm…"

She glanced at his profile, those sharp cheekbones, that strong jaw, a perfect lumberjack model face. "Vince?"

"Yeah?"

"Is this a date?"

"Do you want it to be?"

"I don't know."

"Would it be so bad to go out with me?" he asked in an aggrieved tone.

"You are the enemy."

"Yeah. I'll be honest with you. I'm not big on relationships. So if you want to have a little fun, I'm your guy. If not, then it's just drinks."

"Just drinks, then."

"Fair enough."

She got quiet. Guess putting on her best pushup bra and matching panties had been pointless. Because what happened after a little fun? Awkwardness. An even more tense business relationship. No, thanks.

"Are you sure your anonymous donor friend plays for the other team?" he asked.

"Why would you ask that?"

"Because anyone who coughs up that amount of dough on short notice must have a strong connection to you."

She folded her hands in her lap. "We ended on good terms. We're friends."

"He still wants you."

"I told you we're friends."

"Guys don't stay friends unless they want more action between the sheets."

She scowled. "You mean you don't."

"I mean *all* guys don't."

"You don't know everything."

He smirked. "I know how guys think."

"So do I."

He glanced at her. "I sincerely doubt that."

"I'm very intuitive."

"So what am I thinking right now?"

"You're thinking I can't wait to have a beer."

"You're good."

"Told you."

He stopped at a red light and pinned her with a hot gaze and a slow, sexy smile. Her stomach fluttered. She forced a smile back.

"Am I making you nervous?" he asked. "Because that was a very strange smile you just gave me."

Her leg jiggled. "Not at all."

"Good. You're safe with me."

"Hmmm...."

He hit the accelerator. "Really."

"You rubbed my butt," she reminded him.

"Bah. I was just playing around."

"Don't play with me."

He chuckled. "But you're so much fun to mess with."

"Seriously, don't play with me."

"All right, all right."

They got to the bar, and Vince got them two seats near the big TV. He ordered a platter of wings and a couple of beers. Sophia dove right in. Vince watched the TV. The Sox were on tonight. She watched too. She liked baseball. During a commercial, he turned to her. "Oh, hey, sorry. I got distracted by the game."

"No problem."

"How was your day?" he asked, actually looking interested in her answer.

"Sucky. Putting out fires. Paperwork got lost on a project, and I had to do everything over on an expedited basis." She sipped her beer. "How was your day?"

"Busy. Roofing." He reached over and pressed his thumb to the side of her mouth, surprising her. "Sauce."

"Oh."

He dropped his hand and stared at her mouth. "Hey, you want to finish watching the game at my place?"

"For a little fun?"

His hand snuck up the back of her shirt, stroking her bare lower back. He met her eyes and gave her a slow, sexy smile. "If you want."

"No, thanks."

He dropped his hand. "You want to go home?"

"After the seventh inning."

His eyes widened. "You actually like the game?"

"Yeah." The game came back on, and she returned her attention to the TV.

"Wow," he muttered under his breath. Then he grabbed her and hauled her into his lap. She let out a squeak. His arms wrapped around her waist. "I think you might be my dream girl," he whispered in her ear.

"Vince." She couldn't help but laugh. "Gimme a break." She wiggled to get off his lap, but his hands clamped on her hips, holding her in place.

"Settle down now," he said, resting his chin on her shoulder and watching the game.

She did. And for the first time in a long time she felt light and carefree, held safe in his arms.

12

Sophia met with Vince and the architect at the library for a site inspection. It was early Monday morning. The library wouldn't open for a couple of more hours. She'd have to work late to make it up to her boss, but at least she was working from home most of this week. Soon, they'd need to shut the library down and move the collection to a temporary location. But for now it was as it'd always been—musty and overloaded with books and DVDs.

Vince jerked his chin at her. "Hey."

She jerked her chin, playing the macho guy back. "Hey."

He grinned and shook his head. After they'd watched the game, he'd driven her back home and walked her to the door. She'd given him a firm handshake goodnight, which made him laugh, and then he left. He'd been upfront with her about not wanting a relationship. She took him at his word. So what if she craved him? She could find someone she craved that also wanted a relationship.

Vince rattled off a list of problems with the oldest part of the library to the architect as they moved through the space, starting with the ancient electrical to the crumbling foundation and leaky roof. Nothing she hadn't seen before. She took note of the original pieces they'd like to preserve from the mosaic foyer to the front door and especially the fireplace in the front meeting room. They were working their way through to the back of the library when a voice boomed, "There he is! The prodigal son!"

Sophia whirled to find her dad standing there, hands on his hips, glaring at Vince. Her dad approached, all badass swagger, as much as a man in his sixties could when faced with the likes of a model lumberjack in the muscled perfection of Vince Marino. Vince glanced at her quickly, and she sent him an apologetic look. There were always apologies necessary with her dad. Vince met her dad halfway.

Her dad scowled. "Looking at you is like looking at Vinny." He said "Vinny" like it was an extremely distasteful thing. Her dad with his heavyset brow and protruding jaw was a very manly man, but not pretty. Her mom always said she married him for his oozing sexuality, which made Sophia wish her mom treated her more like a daughter and less like a confidante because, really, who wanted to think of their dad that way?

"Thank you," Vince boomed.

Sophia rushed over. "Dad, what are you doing here? I said I had it handled." Heat crept up her neck. The architect wandered away, giving them privacy.

"Scram, Vince," her dad said, hitching his thumb toward the exit. "I've got it from here."

"I'm lead on this project," Vince said. "I'm not going anywhere."

"Well, now I'm lead. So *get out.*" Her dad was a good six inches shorter than Vince, with a wiry frame, but damn if he wasn't his usual pit bull self.

"Dad, please," Sophia said. "I've got it."

"No, you don't," her dad barked. "Or you wouldn't still be taking orders from this guy." He jabbed a finger at Vince.

"I'm not taking orders," she replied calmly. "We just got here. We're doing a site inspection."

Her dad frowned. "You can go, Sophia." The remark stung. She was good to keep around for some things, like total chaos, but once her usefulness had passed, it was *go away.* She blinked rapidly. She should have expected this.

"Don't talk to her like that," Vince snapped.

Her dad puffed out his chest. "Or what?" And then, hand to God, her dad spat on the floor by Vince's feet in challenge. This was so embarrassing.

Vince ignored it and turned his back on them, continuing with the site inspection with the architect on the other side of the room.

Her dad shook his fist at him. "Coward! I'm calling your dad to see what he thinks about this travesty!"

Vince kept ignoring him. Sophia wanted to shrink into a hole in the floor. Her dad kicked over a plastic recycle can and stormed out.

"Soph, get over here," Vince said. "We need you in the loop."

Her spirits lifted at his casual inclusion of her. She returned to Vince and the architect. "Sorry about that. I'll talk to him."

"It's good you got your mom's looks," Vince said, sparing her a glance.

She laughed despite herself. They finished up their meeting, and Vince walked her out to her car.

He stopped, leaning a hand against the roof of the car. "Don't forget my dad only agreed to this if your dad wasn't involved. Make sure he understands I'm the boss."

"You're not the boss," she countered. "We're sharing the leadership."

"You can think that all you want, but that don't make it true."

"There is no I in team," she said.

He bit back a smile. "My dream girl wouldn't challenge my alpha status."

She grinned. "Maybe I'm not your dream girl."

He stepped back and took her in from head to toe. "I like that skirt."

She heated under his gaze. "Thank you for not getting into it with my dad."

"I pick my battles."

"Smart."

"I'm not known for my smarts."

"What are you known for?"

He tipped her chin up, held it for a moment and leaned close, his breath fanning over her face. "Wouldn't you like to know?"

And then he left, leaving her craving again. Dammit.

Sophia went home from work that night to find her dad back home. The for-sale sign was tossed on the front lawn. She went inside and braced herself.

"I'm not selling the house," he announced.

"Dad, we need the money. And you don't need this big old place."

"How dare you put it up for sale without telling me!"

"I'm the one living here. I'm the one doing everything while you eat pizza and drink beer in your bathrobe. What was I supposed to do?"

"I'm moving back in," he boomed. "You need me to take charge. You are hereby relieved of the Clover Park Library project."

Sophia sighed. "Dad, I'm not leaving the project. I worked out a good deal. Our company working the historic architecture angle, Marino working the new construction angle."

"Marino! No way. We're new construction. There's no angle, Sophia! Whose side are you on?" He paced the living room.

"Our side. Obviously. Who do you think's been working all this time to keep us afloat? All while barely hanging onto my own job. My boss isn't happy with the time I've taken off to get this project off the ground. I'll be lucky if they don't fire me! It's not like you're paying me."

He stopped pacing and looked at her. "Okay, okay. But everything's fine now. I'm back. And Marino's out."

"We signed a contract with them."

He shook his head. "I'll work on that. This baby is ours all the way. As soon as the first payment rolls in, I'll put you on payroll."

She wasn't so sure she wanted to work for her dad full time. "I'll have to think—"

"Have you heard from your mother lately?"

She'd received a series of texts from her mom explaining she wasn't pregnant, but was, in fact, perimenopausal and had merely missed a period. Again, too much information shared. "Yes, she's fine, and she's not pregnant."

Her dad's eyes bugged out. "She's not?"

"No."

He punched a hand in the air. "I'm getting her back!" He headed for the door and then turned back, muttering about a suitcase.

"Dad, don't go to Florida. Please. She seems very set on staying there." With Manuel the hottie poolboy. He was beautiful if you liked gorgeous Brazilian guys with high libidos. Again, too much information from her mom. A visit would only set her dad back. And he'd finally scraped himself off the sofa at his brother's house.

He paced back and forth and finally stopped in front of her. "All right, all right. I'll wait until she misses me more. Back to business. We have to find a way to push Marino out of this project. Think, Sophia."

"Dad," she said patiently, "Capello Construction wouldn't even be viable if they hadn't partnered with us."

"I never agreed to a partnership."

"I did, on your behalf."

"And I suppose Vince did on his dad's behalf?"

"I met with his dad, and he signed off on it."

"I'm calling that yellow-bellied asshole," her dad shouted, heading for the kitchen for the phone. It was the old-fashioned kind from the '80s with a long cord. He didn't like to use his cell phone because he feared it would give him brain cancer. He kept one only for work.

"Dad, please don't. Just let us handle this one. It doesn't have to be a permanent arrangement. Just a trial project."

He held the phone and paused. "Are you sweet on him? His son, I mean."

Her cheeks heated. "It's just a project. But Vince knows what he's doing. More than I do."

"Well, I know what I'm doing too. And I'm back!"

With that, he dialed Vince's dad (he appeared to have the number memorized), hollered for ten minutes straight, then hung up.

"What did he say?" she asked.

"We'll see. I left a message on his work voicemail."

"For ten minutes?" she asked incredulously.

"Well, it beeped, but I figure it has some more time after that. What're you making for dinner?"

"Salad."

"Meh. Fine. Got any prosciutto?"

"Yes, I have prosciutto."

"Fix me a plate? Please."

"You know where the plates are," she said.

He stomped off to the kitchen. She sighed. Maybe she should move back to her place in Brooklyn. Her dad wasn't the easiest man to live with. On the other hand, she did want to work on the Clover Park project, which was easier to do from her parents' house than from Brooklyn. And she'd already invested a good amount of time in what was proving to be an interesting project. Of course, now that her dad was back, she wasn't sure how long they'd still be involved in the job. Her dad wasn't winning any brownie points with the firm that had saved them.

Vince hung up the phone with his dad later that night and rubbed the back of his neck. Ever since Sophia crashed into his life, things had gotten complicated. His dad was irate over a phone call from Joe Capello. It seemed Joe wanted Marino and Sons out, and Vince's dad was digging his heels in and told Vince they weren't dropping this project under any circumstances. They had a signed contract and were moving forward as planned.

He also wanted Vince to push back and get Joe out of the picture. That meant only one thing—appealing to Sophia. He punched in her cell number and told her the situation. Her voice, at once concerned and forthright, made him relax almost immediately. She couldn't help it if her dad was a nut.

"I'm so sorry," she said. "Geez, this is embarrassing. I'll work out something with my dad. He won't derail anything."

"What's your plan to call the pit bull off?"

"I'll think of something. Don't worry. I've had a lot of experience with handling my family."

"Have you given any thought to my proposition?" he asked because it was all he could think about for a week straight.

She paused. "What proposition?"

"Don't play dumb."

"No."

"No, you don't want two nights of fingers-fisting-in-the-sheets, or no, you haven't thought about it anymore?"

"Have you?"

It's all I can think about. "Just now."

"I only thought about it just now too."

"Uh-huh. So what do you think?"

"I think I don't want to be another one of your conquests."

"It's not healthy to keep all that passion pent up inside, Sophia."

Her voice dropped to a whisper. "I don't have pent-up passion."

"You do. Trust me."

"I don't trust you at all."

"Why not?"

"Because you have ulterior motives."

He found himself smiling. "And they are?"

"To sleep with me, obviously."

"And your point is…"

Silence.

"I'm offering you a good deal," he said.

"Fuck that."

He grinned. "You got the first part right."

She hung up. He shook his head. He hadn't meant to piss her off. He was just messing with her. Kind of. It was insane how much he wanted her.

Bah, it was better this way. Sophia had trouble written all over her. She'd expect things outside of the bedroom that he didn't know how to give.

He would disappoint her.

He let out a breath. And wasn't that just the story of his life? Disappointing people. Not measuring up.

But he couldn't stop thinking about her. It was like he'd been infected. And the only cure was Sophia.

13

Sophia had hoped not to have to deal with Vince for a few weeks. He was too good at getting her riled up, and her defenses were weakening the more time she spent with him. It had been twelve long restless nights since he'd propositioned her with two nights of unbridled passion and the idea had, unfortunately, lodged firmly in her mind. She longed for what he described yet knew better than to become just another in a long line of women for him.

Since they were waiting on some permits, and she was still working on moving the historic paperwork through, there was no reason whatsoever for Vince to show up at the library on Saturday. She'd organized some volunteers to move the library's contents to a temporary space in the Episcopal church annex, where the library would operate until construction on the new library was completed.

He wore a T-shirt that stretched across his massive shoulders and chest and tapered down over rock-hard abs to jeans that looked well-worn and molded to his frame. He crossed to her, his confident stride eating up the space between them, and she fought the urge to bolt. Instead she locked her knees against the now familiar surge of lust for his Italian lumberjack good looks. It was the person on the inside that counted. She wanted someone she could have deep, thoughtful conversations with. Not someone that teased her and made her feel like she was missing out just because she'd never rolled around in ecstasy.

He flashed a smile, swooped in and kissed her cheek. "We're here to help."

She flushed and noticed for the first time that Vince had brought a couple of guys with him. "Hi, Nico."

"Hello, *bella*," Nico replied.

A tall man with dirty blond disheveled hair, stubbled jaw, and a dimpled smile offered his hand. "I'm Vince's brother Jared."

"Hi, nice to meet you. Sophia." She turned to Vince. "You didn't have to come today. I've got the Friends of the Library volunteers helping out." She gestured to the twenty or so people boxing up the books and using carts to load them onto a rented moving truck. They'd already put in two hours of very productive work.

Vince slammed his hands on his hips. "I can't believe you didn't consult me on this."

"Why would I?" she asked. "It's not construction."

"Sophia, look around. These are mostly old people." He pointed. "Miss Smith is ancient and under five foot!"

"Shhh!" She grabbed his finger and brought it down. Miss Smith was the retired librarian and, after fifty years of working at the Clover Park Library, had wanted to be included.

Vince shook his head. "You need us, and you're welcome. You can repay me with dinner."

With that, he gestured to his brothers, and they started piling heavy boxes one on top of the other, loading up the carts.

Sophia pulled old volumes of Clover Park records off the shelf and stacked them in a box. Vince passed by and winked at her.

"I'm not buying you dinner, Vince."

"Fine, I'll pay."

She gritted her teeth. Dinner with Vince was just foreplay to him. She refused to be sucked into his seduction game.

He moved off and started directing the volunteers. Soon, he had the older volunteers labeling boxes and taping them up, while the younger, stronger volunteers piled the books up. He and Nico hauled the boxes and piled them on carts. Jared stayed by the truck and arranged things in there. She couldn't deny it was an efficient system, but it was still aggravating the way he just took over.

By lunchtime, they'd made great progress. Sophia ordered pizza and subs for everyone. She'd just put a slice on a paper plate when she heard Vince bellow, "Yo, Sophia, over here."

She set her teeth. He was so…just so…Vince. She slowly turned. "What?"

He patted the floor next to him. "Come sit with me."

Several of the volunteers watched with interest. "I'm okay."

He raised his brows. "Don't make me come get you!" he boomed.

Some people tittered. Her cheeks burned. Nico laughed and elbowed her. "He can't help it. Go teach him some manners."

Head held high, she walked over to where he sat and stared down at him. "In the future, I'd appreciate a nice invitation. Sophia, would you like to join me? Sophia, have some lunch with me. I saved you a spot. Not 'Yo, Sophia' across the room. Not a threat to come get me."

He eyed her. "Are you done?"

She thought about it. "Yes."

"Sit your ass down here." He was already reaching for her plate and bottled water. "Please."

She heaved a sigh and sat on the floor next to him.

"I'm not some pansy-ass boyfriend you can order around, so you might as well give up." He took a bite of pizza that took in half the slice.

"Nico told me to teach you some manners," she said. "He's right."

"Forget about Nico," he said around the pizza stuffed in his mouth. He chewed and swallowed quickly. "No way in hell he's touching you."

"Not every conversation is foreplay. But I have a feeling he would actually ask me out nicely, not proposition me like some ill-mannered men."

Vince chuckled. "Still thinking that one over?"

"No," she replied quickly. She took a bite of pizza and tried very hard to ignore Vince's long, thickly muscled leg pressed up against hers. Her jeans were no match for resisting that kind of heat. She shifted away.

Vince shifted closer, now touching from hip to knee, and leaned down to her ear. "Why didn't you call me about this?" he asked quietly. "I had to find out when I ran into the mayor and he asked how many people I could bring. Didn't you think I'd come through?" He sounded almost hurt.

"No. I just, well, it's not a paying gig, and I didn't want to bother you with it. I already had volunteers."

"If I'd had more notice, I could've gotten more guys."

He straightened and took a long drink of water. She watched his Adam's apple going up and down that thick neck. Why did that turn her on? He was just so thick, so massive, so…solid. Unlike any of the men she'd dated.

He turned to her, and his deep brown eyes locked with hers. "I may not be your ideal guy in terms of, I dunno, sophistication, but I'm a guy you can count on. You need me for something, I'm there. No questions asked."

Her throat felt tight. No man had ever been there for her. Not her dad, not her brother, not any of her pansy-ass boyfriends. "That's, um, nice."

One corner of his mouth lifted. "It's not nice. It's just a fact. Thought you should know." Then he grabbed his empty plate and water bottle and stood. "Back to work."

She found herself watching him walk away. The confident stride, the broad back, the tight ass. He was magnificent.

He looked over his shoulder, caught her looking, and grinned. "I'm looking forward to our dinner tonight."

"You get lunch," she said. "And you just ate it."

"We'll see." Then he swaggered off.

How could she argue with that? He didn't take no for an answer. What did he want to go to dinner for anyway? She'd told him she didn't want a one- or two-night stand. He didn't want a relationship. What was the point of dinner? She finished her lunch and went back to work.

Nico chatted with her frequently, smiling and joking around. He was funny and charming. But she kept feeling Vince's eyes burning a hole into her, and she couldn't completely relax.

Finally they finished getting everything into the church annex. They'd come back tomorrow to unload the boxes there for the temporary library. She and her volunteers were beat. It was quite a project. Some of the collection went into storage. Vince supervised that too, driving off to the storage space with his brothers to help unload there.

She went home strangely disappointed that he'd seemed to have forgotten all about dinner.

Vince showed up at Sophia's house an hour later with dinner in a takeout bag. He probably should've showered first, but he was in a hurry to get to her before she ate dinner on her own, and then he'd have no excuse for being there.

Sophia opened the door, eyes wide. "Vince! What're you doing here?"

He held up the bag. "You owe me dinner."

She stared at him. He checked out her loose V-neck shirt, leggings, and bare feet. Pajamas?

"Did you eat yet?" he asked.

"No, I just got out of the shower."

He brushed past her, and her spicy rose scent wafted around him. He stopped when she didn't follow him. She crossed her arms, hugging her middle. Like she was nervous being alone with him.

"Sophia, you're safe with me. Promise." He would never force himself on a woman. "I was just teasing with that proposition." Sort of.

She lifted her chin. "I wasn't worried. I was just surprised to see you. I thought I said no to dinner."

"And I said yes. Where's the kitchen?"

She heaved a sigh and led the way. He followed behind, watching how her long hair caught the light, shades of caramel and chocolate. Damn, he was hungry.

"What'd you get?" she asked as she took out plates.

"Someone recommended Pete's Fish and Chips."

She turned. "Did you get the lobster rolls?"

He grinned. "Yup. Had to get what they're famous for."

"Omigod, I love you!" He jolted at the strange sensation in his chest. He'd never heard the L word directed at him from anyone but family. She sat across from him, grabbed her sandwich from the bag, tore off the wrapper, and took a big bite. She closed her eyes in lobster-roll ecstasy. "Mmm…so good."

Vince adjusted himself discreetly. Something strangely erotic about the way she ate that lobster roll.

She opened her eyes. "Aren't you going to eat?"

"Yeah." He sat across from her, quickly unwrapped his sandwich, and took a bite. "Pretty good."

"Good, it's awesome! You won't get better than this. Pete always makes them fresh with deliveries straight from Maine." She took another bite and rolled her eyes orgasmically. He wanted to look away, but he was caught in thrall. She closed her eyes again, and he just watched her, fantasizing about her in bed, her long hair spread out on the pillow, moaning, writhing—

He stood abruptly and started searching the cabinets for a glass. He filled it with ice and poured water.

"You okay?" she asked. "You barely ate anything."

"Fine," he barked. He stood a distance away and guzzled down the ice water.

She lifted one shoulder up and down, and the sleeve shifted, revealing smooth glowing skin. No bra strap. His gaze immediately dropped to her chest. They seemed covered. Maybe some strapless pushup bra. This had been a dumb idea. The two of them alone at her place.

He returned to the table and wolfed down his sandwich. "Thanks for dinner. I better go."

She smiled. "I should be thanking you for dinner. Where are you heading in such a hurry? Hot date?"

"No," he barked. Then he crumpled up his trash and searched for the garbage. He had to get out of here before he pushed his luck. How did guys manage this dating thing? The lust was overpowering. He was used to just going for it.

She licked her fingers clean. He broke out in a sweat.

She smiled at him. "You want to watch the playoff game? We've got a really cool theater room. It's in a loft. Big-screen TV, recliner chairs, huge beanbags. I could make popcorn."

The Sox had made it to the playoffs. Of course he wanted to watch it. He'd nearly forgotten about it in his rush to get to her. He wasn't entirely sure how much of the game he'd actually see alone in a loft with her, still…she'd invited him to stay. He'd barged in here demanding dinner, but now it felt like she was into the date thing too.

He raised a brow. "So this *is* a date."

She crumpled up her sandwich wrapper. "I thought you didn't date."

"I don't."

"Then it isn't." She stood and cleared her dishes. "Forget it."

He came up behind her at the sink. He wanted nothing more than to wrap his arms around her waist, push that long hair out of the way, and taste the side of her neck. But he didn't touch her. Not at all. Because he didn't know how to without going all out. Seduction was easy. Just being with her was the most difficult thing he'd ever done.

"Sophia." He loved her name.

"What?" she asked softly.

"I would love to watch the playoffs with you."

"As friends?"

"No."

She let out a shaky breath, and he let himself touch her, stroking her long hair over one shoulder. The pulse point in her neck drew him in, and he placed a soft kiss there. Her head tilted, a silent offering, and he took full advantage, kissing along the column of her throat, hot, open-mouthed kisses, tasting her, all roses and spice and Sophia. She turned in his arms and looked up at him, eyes soft, cheeks flushed, lips parted. He leaned down to claim her mouth when her hand slammed against his chest.

"I will have this date with you if there is nothing physical," she said.

"What? You liked that." He snagged her around the waist, his hands resting lightly on her. "Don't tell me you didn't."

"It was pleasant."

He dropped his hands. "Pleasant!"

"And after this one nonphysical date, I won't be calling you. You have to call me. Only if you want a second nonphysical date."

He couldn't believe it. What kind of dating was this? He might as well be hanging out with his brothers. Did she not like when he kissed her neck? He studied her. Her cheeks were pink. Definitely not unaffected by him.

"But the physical stuff is the fun part," he said on a near groan.

She crossed her arms. "Those are my terms."

"When was the last time you slept with someone?"

"When was the last time you slept with someone?" she fired back.

"I stopped when I met you." Shit. He hadn't meant to show his cards like that.

"Vince," she said, "really?" Her arms looped around his waist. At least she was touching him.

"No one could compare," he admitted, hoping she'd touch him some more.

She leaned her cheek against his chest and hugged him. His arms wrapped around her. She sighed. It felt surprisingly good just to hold her.

She pulled back and looked up at him. How was he not supposed to claim that delectable mouth? And that body.

"Vince, that's so sweet. Is that true?"

"Course it's true," he grumbled.

She hugged him again, looking entirely too happy about his celibate state. It was embarrassing. He wished it weren't true. He'd even tried to pick up someone at a bar, but all he could see was Sophia and her fiery nature.

He set her away from him. "No more hugging. You're turning me into a pansy."

"Sorry." She grinned cheekily.

"You owe me some passion for that." He was hungry for her, craving her, and all this hugging was just making the need to have her more sharp. A damn urgency. Fighting it felt wrong. "Come on. You can give me something. Please." He felt like such a wimp for begging like this, but he was powerless, caught in her spell. "One kiss."

She held up a finger. "No hands."

"You're a tough negotiator," he said as he backed her into the wall and pressed against her. He didn't need hands. His lips and tongue and teeth could do all he wanted. He kissed her, his hands against the wall on either side of her, boxing her in. She wrapped her arms around his neck. He nipped her lower lip, making her gasp, and thrust his tongue in her delicious mouth. He kissed her with all the pent-up passion he had from the moment they met, and she moaned in the back of her throat. She was rocking her hips into him, maybe not even aware she was doing it, but he was damn pleased. He ground against her.

The front door opened and slammed shut. "Soph, you home?" a voice called.

Sophia bolted upright. She pushed at his chest. "It's my dad. He can't see you here. Go out the back door."

He glanced over at the back door. "I'm sure he saw my car."

"Soph? You got company?" her dad called.

"We have to keep this secret!" she hissed. "I'll cover for you. Go!"

He backed up a step, so he wasn't plastered against her, but no way he was slinking out the back door like some juvenile delinquent.

Her dad stopped short in the kitchen and narrowed his eyes. "What the hell are you doing here?"

"We just finished dinner," Vince said.

"Get out of my house!" her dad hollered.

"Dad!" Sophia exclaimed.

Vince turned to Sophia. "I'll call you."

Sophia grimaced. "He means for work. We were helping out at the library today, moving the collection."

"You'd better stay away from my daughter!" her dad roared. He shook a fist at Vince.

"See ya, Soph," Vince said, leaning down to kiss her cheek. He spoke softly in her ear. "I like no hands."

"What's he saying?" her dad thundered.

Sophia smoothed her hair over her ear. "Y-yes. That sounds good."

He could hear her dad hollering some more, but he didn't care. It had been one hell of a kiss, and he could do a lot more with no hands. He would do a lot more.

14

Vince picked Sophia up the following Saturday night for their second date. He planned on taking her bowling, something he was good at. He'd debated between that and the batting cages, she did like baseball, but went with bowling because they could get a bite to eat at the same time.

She opened the door, wearing a purple strapless dress with a little white wrap around her shoulders. She looked so beautiful. Too beautiful. Like she was going someplace classy with a classy guy.

"Your dad home?" he asked, figuring it was best to be prepared.

"No."

"Where did you think we were going?" he asked.

"I didn't know. You said someplace nice with food."

He hung his head. What the hell was she doing with a guy like him? And how could he ask her to change? He stared at her beautiful delicate feet in black stilettos. Those feet didn't belong in rented bowling shoes.

"Vince? Are you okay?"

He met her eyes. "Why did you say yes to tonight?"

"I had a nice time on our first nonphysical date."

He grunted.

She smiled. "Even though you cheated and kissed me."

"But no hands," he pointed out.

"No hands," she agreed.

He rocked back and forth on his heels. He wore a T-shirt and jeans. It was a new T-shirt, but still. He felt really stupid at this mismatch in their plans and expectations. Obviously he didn't know the first thing about dating a woman like Sophia. "What kind of dates are you used to going on?"

"Is something wrong?"

"I think…" He backed away. "I think maybe you got the wrong guy."

"What do you mean? Where are you going?"

"I'm letting you off the hook."

She stamped her foot. "The hell you are. You asked me out, and you're taking me out."

He stopped. "I planned on taking you bowling. Maybe get some beer and nachos." He gestured to her outfit. "Nothing this pretty. Nothing like you deserve."

She slipped off her heels, turned, and went back in the house. Guess she agreed. The door shut quietly behind her, and he headed down the sidewalk.

"Yo, Vince!"

He froze and a smile broke out. He turned.

She leaned out the front door. "Get your ass in here. Sit tight while I change."

He cocked his head. "You sure?"

"Whadda ya need an engraved invitation?" she asked, sounding a lot like him.

He strode up the steps, his heart filled with hope and something altogether tender. He cupped her jaw with one hand and stroked his thumb over her soft cheek. "You got it."

Bowling with Sophia was a riot. She was terrible, but even if she only got one pin down she did a little victory dance, whooping it up. Almost made his strikes feel like a nonevent. She drank his beer and stole the best pieces of nachos with the most cheese on them. He was having a blast until the drive home when she hit him with some very unwelcome news.

"So you know how we're going to have a much bigger space for the new library?" she asked.

"Yeah, I know. I'm the one building it."

"With my help."

He grunted. The groundbreaking ceremony was in three weeks, and he couldn't wait for his dad to see him there with a big sign that said Marino and Sons Construction. He'd ordered two signs for the front and side of the library property to serve as advertisements for their company.

Sophia went on. "Well, we're going to need more books for the collection, which means more money, and my donor friend, Armie, thought a gala dinner would be a great way to raise the money. To be honest, I think he just wants his name on the event. He needs some good publicity after some video got out of him throwing potato chips at tourists after a drunken night at a club. Don't ask."

"Armie who?"

"Armie Zephyr." Vince recognized the name. He was a young actor who'd been lucky enough to score a major role in a new superhero franchise. "My anonymous donor decided not to be anonymous. He's the one that made the big library donation."

"You mean the guy that plays for the other team after sleeping with you."

She huffed. "I mean the actor I dated briefly."

"He threw chips?"

"Yes. Some tourists wanted him to do his signature kick move, you know from the *Blue Metro* movies?"

"Yeah, I know."

"And he hates doing it in real life. Says he feels like a trained monkey putting on a show." She blew out a breath. "I know, it's stupid. Anyway, he wants me as his date. Just for show."

"Maybe he's bi. Maybe he's still into you."

"That's over. I just thought I'd mention it since we're

kinda…seeing each other. A little. Maybe it doesn't matter. Maybe you're sick of me."

"I'm not sick of you."

"Oh. Okay."

"When is this gala dinner?" And where's my invitation? Didn't she think he could handle himself at a classy gala event?

"Three weeks after the groundbreaking."

His temper flared because she still didn't invite him. In fact, she was just humming along to the radio like it didn't even matter. He drummed his fingers on the steering wheel and clenched his jaw tight so he wouldn't yell. Finally when he pulled into her driveway, he asked her point-blank in as calm a voice as he could muster, "Am I invited?"

"Oh, did you want to go? I didn't think it was your kind of thing. Armie and I thought we'd invite people who were, you know, big spenders. It's a fundraiser."

"How much are the tickets?" he asked through clenched teeth.

"A thousand dollars. Black tie. I only mentioned it so you wouldn't worry. Armie and I are just friends."

"Yeah, I heard that part."

"You can go if you want. We'll waive the fee. I just didn't think you'd want to."

"No, why would I want to? Why would the guy who builds the damn library care what goes in it? It's not like I read, right?"

Her eyes widened. "What're you getting so worked up about? It's just a boring dinner. I told you as a courtesy."

"Courtesy. Yeah. Save your fancy manners for Armie."

"I don't understand what you're upset about. Are you jealous?"

"No."

"Did you feel left out?"

"No."

"Then what?"

How could he explain that he was out of her league? Maybe she was better off with pansy-ass boyfriends who would actually like going to black-tie events and spouting historical facts. Maybe that was what turned her on.

Still, she'd said she'd never got off on any of them.

"You slumming with me, Sophia?" he finally asked.

"I have no idea what you're talking about."

"I didn't go to college. I don't do black tie. You said you had to teach me manners."

"Nico said that. And he's right."

His shoulders slumped. She rubbed his arm. "I don't care about that other stuff. I've met some real assholes with PhDs. What matters is what's on the inside." Her hand slid across his chest and stopped over his rapidly beating heart. "You have a good heart, Vince."

His eyes watered. Dammit. He put his hand over hers, his throat tight. He had no words and, even if he did, he couldn't get them out.

She leaned close, her breast pressing into his arm, and then she kissed him on the cheek. "Call me for date number three."

He turned to her. She seriously wanted to go out with him again? After he took her bowling instead of to a black-tie event? "Are you sure?"

"Damn hell sure." She was so cute when she cursed.

A smile dawned slowly. "Third date could get physical."

She gave him a sexy smile and kissed him, her tongue darting out and touching his. He took control of the kiss, like a starving man feasting on her mouth. Sweet and hot and his, all his.

He pulled back. "There will be hands," he warned. "Mine. All over you."

He kissed her again, had barely gotten started, when she pulled away.

"If you insist," she said. She opened the door and got out.

"Oh, I insist," he called.

She leaned in the open window and gave him a brilliant smile. His heart stopped and then started again, lurching painfully on. "Night, Vince."

"Night. Wait. Let me walk you to the door." He took off his seatbelt, belatedly remembering his manners.

"Don't. My dad's home now. I'm really not up to a confrontation. He said he'd get his bat if you showed your face here again."

"Bloodthirsty."

"That's him, not me." She blew him a kiss and damn if he didn't catch it.

15

───────

Sophia got ready for her third date with Vince, humming with nerves. She knew him well enough after a month to know he meant it when he said things would get physical. And when he promised he'd show her ecstasy, she believed him. She couldn't wait, actually. She was realistic about it, though, didn't expect he'd want much to do with her after tonight. She'd insisted on a few nonphysical dates because she needed to ease into the physical. And she didn't want him to think her slutty even though his words, "fingers fisting in the sheets, raw, screaming-top-of-your-lungs orgasm" had run on repeat in her head ever since he'd uttered them.

She had to know what she'd been missing all these years.

For her sex had always been slightly awkward and over before she even had a chance to get into it. She wore her hair down, put on her favorite purple lace bra and panty set, and went with her trusty little black dress. She knew he liked her in dresses.

Whatever happened after tonight, it would be okay, she told herself as she carefully applied makeup. She and Vince were rarely on site at the library at the same time. She'd turned in her plans for preserving the historic section. Most of the rest of the job was in Vince's hands. He would be busy doing assessment and testing before the demolition of the old space that had been added on in the 1960s.

She'd be moving back to her apartment in Brooklyn soon. She had a new client in the city and it was time for her to pay attention to her real job before she lost it. Her dad was permanently back home, so she wasn't needed to watch over the house. And she missed her old social life. She didn't have any friends left here in Greenport, and night after night sitting home with only her dad for company had gotten old fast. Her weekly date with Vince was the highlight of her week. Not that she'd ever tell him that. Let him think she was having a grand time without him.

The doorbell rang, and she hurried to answer it before her dad could threaten Vince with bodily harm. It would be hard to enjoy herself if the night started off with total embarrassment.

"I got it," she called. Tonight they'd be going to a nice Italian restaurant in Eastman, Vince's idea. He lived in Eastman, so it would be a short drive to his place, and she was eager to finally see the upstairs of the old carriage house he called home.

"Who is it?" her dad called.

"Don't wait up, Dad. I'm spending the night at a friend's place."

"What friend?"

She dashed out the door.

"Hey," Vince said, swallowing visibly and giving her the once-over. "You look amazing."

"Thanks. You too." He wore a navy blue suit minus the blazer. She put a hand on his arm. "Let's go before my dad comes out here."

He put his hand over hers, holding her arm, led her to his car, and opened the door for her.

"Such manners," she teased.

"I can take a hint," he said with a smile. His gaze was warm and tender, and she found herself basking in that smile. Like he adored her and only her. *Don't go thinking crazy.* Vince had been very upfront about what it meant to get involved with him.

"How was your week?" he asked after he got in the car.

"Good. I'm still waiting to hear on the historic paperwork for the library. I'm working on a church in the city that has a very old bell tower they want to preserve."

"Cool."

"Yeah, it is, actually. How about you?"

"Can't complain."

"And how's your family? How's your godson?" She always liked to hear about his brothers and what was going on in their lives. And she knew he loved to talk about the baby.

He beamed. "Family's good. My godson is growing, moving like crazy. He kicks his ma so hard. He's going to be an athlete."

"I'm sure you'll be a great godfather."

He got quiet. She looked out the window at the passing scenery, surprised at how calm she was, given what she expected to happen tonight.

"You want kids, Sophia?"

She snapped her head around, shocked at the question coming from him of all people—the good-time guy. "Sure, someday. If I met the right man, got married. You know, the whole deal. How about you?"

He didn't reply. He was probably hoping she didn't want them. Too much ball and chain there. Still, he was excited about his godson. Why had he asked that? She couldn't quite figure him out.

They went to dinner, and Vince was extremely polite and respectful. It was a little unnerving. She felt like she was on a date with someone she didn't know. Gone was the teasing, the gruff affection. He held doors open for her, helped her off with her coat, held out her chair, inquired what she'd like to eat and then ordered for her.

"Is everything okay?" she asked.

"Why do you ask?"

"You're being almost too polite."

"First I need to learn manners and now I'm too polite. What do you want from me?"

"I just want you to be yourself."

"I'm not getting that vibe from you at all." He scowled. "I'm trying really hard to stop being dumb old Vince."

"You're not dumb!" She thought quickly. She couldn't let everything fall apart before she even had a chance to experience the passion he'd promised her. "Please don't be mad. I've really been looking forward to tonight."

He crossed those big muscular arms, the fabric straining across his bulging biceps. "Why?"

She licked her lips nervously and lowered her voice. "Because of what you mentioned before."

He dropped his arms and leaned across the table. "Gimme a clue. I'm new to all this. And the female mind is a little mysterious."

"The fingers-fisting-in-the-sheets thing," she whispered.

He jolted. Then he looked side to side around the restaurant.

She took a long drink of wine, watching him. He turned back to her, his deep brown eyes burning into hers. "You sure about this, Soph?"

She nearly sagged in relief. "Yes, I'm sure. Very sure."

He took her hand, lifted it, and placed a warm kiss on the back of her hand. "I can't wait."

Sophia surprised Vince tonight. She'd been so careful to keep him in check. He could hardly believe that on their third date she was ready for more. Hell, what did he know? Maybe third date was always when she slept with someone. He never made it past the first date, unless the woman called him for a repeat performance. Even then it was twice and done. Third time had never happened. He'd never wanted it to happen, but Sophia was different. Yes, she was beautiful, but it was more than that. She was smart with all her history knowledge, a real lady, a classy lady, but with a fiery passionate nature. He still didn't know what she wanted with the likes of him, but he was happy to go along with it.

They finished dinner, and she got quiet. Maybe she was having second thoughts.

He walked her out the door and to his car. "You know, Soph, we don't have to…I'm fine with—"

She turned and put two fingers over his lips. "Don't try to talk me out of it. My mind is made up."

He studied her and saw the bluster for what it was. She was nervous. He grabbed her fingers and kissed them. "Let's go."

She let out a shaky breath. Geez, what did she think he was going to do to her? It was just a roll in the hay. He wasn't into any kinky stuff. He guided her into the car and headed home.

She was so unusually quiet and tense on the drive back that he pulled out a whopper of a lie just to calm her the frick down. "I'm bringing you back to my place, but we're just going to talk. Maybe have a glass of wine. Then I'll drive you home."

"If you do that, I'll never speak to you again!" she hollered.

He barked out a laugh.

"I mean it!"

"Okay, okay."

"Fingers fisting in the sheets!" she demanded, making him feel damn giddy. She might be nervous, but she sure was determined. Far be it from him to deny a woman like Sophia what she wanted.

"All right, all right, you talked me into it."

"Good."

He bit back a smile. Once they got back to his place, Sophia wandered around his living room, touching the stone on the old fireplace, looking all around at everything but him. He crossed to her, helped her off with her coat, and hung it on a hook by the door. Then she was on the move again, inspecting everything in the room. Normally he just headed straight upstairs with whoever he brought home. He didn't want to be like that with Sophia.

"I'll get the wine," he said.

She startled like she'd forgotten he was there. "Okay, thank you."

Slow was the way to go. She wanted it, she just had to be eased into it. He headed for the kitchen, uncorked a bottle of merlot Angel had brought for a family get-together at Vince's place, and poured them each a glass. He returned to the living room and nearly dropped the wine.

Sophia stood there in just a purple lace strapless bra, panties, and those fuck-me stilettos. "I'm waiting," she purred.

"Fuck," he muttered, quickly setting down the wine.

He closed the space between them, wrapped his arms around her, and kissed her. She sank against him all soft, satiny skin, tasting faintly of the wine from dinner and pure sin. His pulse thundered in his ears. His hand slid under her leg, lifting it, opening her to him. The moment his pelvis connected with hers, she moaned, and he just lost it. Consumed with a driving need to have her, his mouth fused with hers while his hands roamed all over, as he'd longed to do since he'd first met her. She clung to him, her tongue tangling with his, and he lifted her. She wrapped her arms and legs around him, and he took her straight upstairs to his bed.

He set her down gently while he hurried to catch up with her, undoing his tie, unbuttoning his shirt, but his fingers were fumbling because Sophia's hands were all over him. Across his chest, down his tight stomach, drifting lower to undo his belt. He jerked, already feeling like he was going to lose it. He grabbed her hand and backed away a step. "Take off your bra," he ordered.

She did. Holy hell. Her breasts were full, the nipples beaded tight. "Vince, I want to touch you."

He quickly shed the rest of his clothes and joined her on the bed. "Let me touch you. Let me show you what you crave." He didn't wait for an answer, merely pressed his mouth to hers, hot and greedy, while his hand shifted down to cup her full breast. His finger rasped over the tight nipple, and she moaned into his mouth. Slow, he told himself even as his body urged him to take hard and fast. Her hips moved restlessly. He kissed his way down her throat to her breast, which he sucked hard and deep. Her hips came off the mattress. Damn, she was responsive. How could passion be new to her?

He turned to the other breast, giving it the same treatment while his fingers rolled and tugged her other nipple. She was moaning, her hands digging into his hair, her hips restless. He slid his hand down her soft belly, let his finger dip under the waistband of her panties, teased her with a soft touch along the entire waistband. She yanked her panties down and off. Couldn't get a clearer signal than that. His fingers delved into hot, wet folds, and she cried out. Sweat broke out on his forehead because he'd never wanted so badly to thrust into oblivion. But he wouldn't rush this. He'd promised Sophia. He wanted her to feel more than she'd ever felt and know it was all because of him.

He removed his hand and returned to kissing her, lying on his side. She rolled to her side, hooking an arm and leg over him, pulling at him, trying to make him roll on top of her. He would've laughed if he wasn't in such a desperate state. He shoved a hand in her hair and held her head, waiting for her to open her eyes. She slowly opened them, her eyes soft and unfocused.

"Soph, this is gonna be slow. This is gonna be roll-your-eyes-back-in-your-head slow, so I suggest you lie back—" he pushed her flat on her back "—and take it."

She whimpered and reached for him again. He took her hands, entwined his fingers with hers, and raised them above her head, pinning them there. Then he proceeded to kiss her from her forehead to her closed eyelids, her soft cheeks, her jawline, and finally he took her mouth. She opened with a soft sigh. Nothing had ever felt so good.

He released her hands and kissed his way down her body, using his hands and mouth to touch every part of her, but especially her breasts and inner thigh, where he teased her before settling between her legs and sucking her hard nub into his mouth. Her hips shot off the bed, and he took advantage, sliding his hands under her ass and holding her there. She got loud then, moaning and calling his name, which only spurred him on. She tasted like honey, and he couldn't get enough. Her nails dug into his shoulders. He stopped and looked up at her, blowing softly over her sex.

"Grab those sheets now," he told her because it felt like she was going to draw blood from his shoulders.

Her fingers immediately fisted in the sheets. He felt a certain sense of pride he'd given her exactly what she'd wanted, and then he pushed her for more because he didn't want just soft whimpers and his name from her. He wanted everything—full-throated screaming in ecstasy. He gentled his touch, his mouth exploring near where she wanted, but not quite. His fingers trailed lower, circling around her opening. She clenched and unclenched in response, and then he finally slid his fingers inside.

"Vince!" she hollered. More like a demand.

He smiled against her. Then he placed soft kisses up and down her, pausing to lick in broad heavy strokes while his fingers did a slow in and out. She started trembling.

He paused to look at her—head thrown back, eyes closed, her hands fisted in the sheets, her hips lifted, silently begging for her release. He'd never seen anything so beautiful. "Sophia."

"Vince!" she hollered. "So help me, if you don't—"

He shut her up, using his lips and tongue and teeth, had just barely gotten started when she screamed and bucked against his mouth. Damn, that was fast. But he didn't release her because feeling her come against his mouth, so thoroughly, so helplessly, only made him want more. He kept going, kissing and licking at her as she quivered underneath him.

"Vince, Vince, I came," she moaned.

He grinned, like he didn't know that. "Now you're going to come again."

"Oh-h-h," she said in a shaky voice. Then he pressed his mouth firmly to her again, and she yelped. He gentled his touch, and she went crazy, writhing and moaning. "Oh, oh, oh."

He looked up to find her fingers fisted in the sheets again. Good. He kept going for himself as much as her. He couldn't get enough of the taste of her. She came violently, bucking against him and screaming his name. He placed one last kiss to her sex, and she moaned and curled up on her side.

He gave her a break to get the condom. Then he joined her on the bed and nudged her so she rolled to her back. "Open those legs, darling."

She did right away, not even opening her eyes. After how much he'd worked her over, her immediate response to open to him again made his heart squeeze. He stroked her hair, silently thanking her for that, before he rose up over her and kissed that luscious mouth just as he thrust deep inside. She gasped into his mouth. He stilled. He probably should've taken that slow, but she'd seemed so ready. "You okay?"

She opened her eyes. They were glazed over with passion. "I'm more than okay," she said in a throaty sultry voice that made him pulse inside her.

He moved slow and deep, trying to draw it out for as long as he could. Their gazes locked, and he felt like he was going to drown in those deep brown eyes. They took him in, held him, loved him. He moved faster, overwhelmed by the depths of his feelings, and closed his eyes. Her nails scraped down his back and when she grabbed his ass, he lost control, pounding into her.

"Come again," he urged.

He lifted her hips as he thrust. He shook with the need to release, and then she cried out, and he let go, shuddering and pumping several more times until he felt emptied out. He lay there for a moment, still shaken by the whole experience, and then took his weight on his forearms so he wouldn't crush her. She just lay there, eyes closed, arms and legs thrown out to her sides in complete abandon, making him smile.

He rolled off her and let out a long breath. He felt incredibly good. Usually he just had a few moments of oblivion, but this was something else. Some powerful afterglow. He took her hand and laced his fingers with hers.

"You were right," she said.

"About what?" He could barely speak after that.

"You did know what you were doing."

He barked out a laugh.

She rolled to her side and propped up on his chest. "What's so funny?"

"Nothing. You knew what you were doing too."

"All I did was lie back and take it like you told me to. You did all the good stuff."

He opened his eyes, wanting her to understand that this was more than just his technique. Her hair was mussed, her cheeks flushed, her lips slightly swollen from his kisses. Unbelievably, his cock stirred. "Soph, it's never been that good. That was us."

"Really?" She sounded like she didn't believe him.

"Something's different about it with you."

She settled her cheek against his chest, and he wrapped an arm around her. "What?" she asked.

He struggled for the words. He didn't know exactly what it was, it just was. "I don't know."

She lifted her head. "I should go."

"Stay. Please." He wasn't done with her. Not by a long shot. "This wasn't a one-night stand."

Her lips formed a flat line. "I know. Two nights."

He groaned. "No. Soph—"

"Three."

"Stop counting. Just—" He pushed her head down on his chest and held her close and tight. "Stop," he finished.

She stayed very still, and he held his breath. Finally she slipped an arm over his chest and her leg curled over his. He rested his hand on her head, stroking her hair back from her face. She let out a soft sigh that made his chest ache. He held her for a while, until her breathing deepened, and only then did he relax, knowing she was going to stay.

16

Sophia woke the next morning, Saturday, with a satisfied smile. Vince had come through as promised. She stretched. He'd even woken her in the middle of the night for another explosive orgasm. He was amazing. A whole new world opened up to her, and she planned to take full advantage. He'd said it wasn't a one-night stand. She opened her eyes and caught Vince heading out the door, gym bag in hand. Her giddy feelings vanished.

She sat up and glanced at the clock. It was only eight thirty. "Where are you rushing off to on a Saturday?"

He stopped and looked guilty. "Nowhere. I just have someplace I gotta be."

She eyed the gym bag. "Can't skip one workout, huh? Muscles too important?" *More important than me,* she added silently.

He laughed. "Yeah. See ya. Oh, hey." He pulled out his wallet and set a couple of twenties on the nightstand. "For cab fare." He shook his head. "Almost forgot. Call me, okay?"

"I won't."

"Fine, I'll call you."

She flopped back down. "Don't bother."

She squeezed her eyes shut tight over the stinging threat of tears. She wouldn't give him the satisfaction. She should have known he'd treat her as casually as any of his conquests. He was just trying to sweet-talk her last night.

The bed creaked under Vince's weight as he sat next to her. He gave her a smacking kiss on the mouth. "I'll see you tonight."

She scowled at him.

"Are you mad?" he asked.

"No, Vince, I love when men race out the door after they sleep with me."

"I'm not racing. I told you I have to be someplace."

"Where?"

He stood and grabbed his bag. "I'll call you."

She threw a pillow at him. "I want some sweet talk! Maybe a few cuddles after a night like that."

He blew out a breath and looked to the ceiling. Finally he met her eyes. "I held you for seven minutes last night."

Her jaw dropped. "Were you watching the clock?"

"It was in my line of vision!"

Grr.

"Look, Soph, if you want round two, then I'll see you tonight."

"That's what you tell all the girls," she spat.

"What do you want from me? I let you spend the night. I never let anyone spend the night."

She propped up on an elbow. "So you just take them home right after?"

"Yeah."

"Are they mad?"

"No."

"How do you know?"

"They didn't say they were mad."

Was he really that clueless? "Were they quiet?"

"Heh." He smirked. "I wear them out."

She was so beyond petty jealousy of his prior women. She was fascinated that he could be this dense. Vince, the confident player, had no clue about women. Zero.

"Do they slam the car door?" she asked.

"Nah. I open the door for them and shut it for them. Why?"

"Then what happens?"

"Then I walk them to the door and tell them to call if they want round two."

She got out of bed and was smugly satisfied to see him take in her naked state with a hungry gaze. She crossed to his side. "Show me."

He groaned and wrapped an arm around her waist, pulling her flush against his body. "Soph, you're not like them."

"Do it! Exactly like you do."

He rolled his eyes. He huffed and puffed. What a man.

"Fine." He put his hand on her waist and walked her to the bedroom door. He stopped. "I had a great time, Sophia." He kissed her quickly. "Call me if you want round two." He patted her on the butt and walked away.

"What was the pat on the butt for?" she asked incredulously.

"You know. Good job. Like in basketball when someone scores or makes a good play."

"Hmm…how many call you for round two?"

He shrugged.

"Ten? Fifteen?"

"I dunno. Maybe three called." He crossed his arms. Was he blushing? The tips of his ears were red. He grabbed his bag and jerked his chin. "I'll call you, okay?"

"Not okay."

He dropped his bag and stalked toward her. She let out a squeak and rushed back toward the bed. He caught up with her, pinned her on the mattress by the shoulders, and kissed her. He pulled back. "I'm calling you, Soph. This isn't over."

"Don't you dare pat my butt."

He grinned. The next thing she knew she was face down on the mattress, one beefy hand holding her down by the shoulder. He gave her butt a pat. "You liked the butt rub to seal the deal." Now his hand was stroking her bottom.

"Did not."

"Why are you so hot, then?"

"Argh!"

And then he left her there, hot and bothered and alone.

Fool me once, Sophia thought bitterly. She was back in Vince's bed Sunday morning after another crazy night of passion, and Vince had once again snuck out early. No note, no goodbye. Just gone. At least she'd taken her car here, so no twenty-dollar bills on the nightstand. She groaned. This was her own fault. Just because she'd never felt anything like the sex they had. She dressed quickly and went downstairs just in time to see Vince take off down the driveway, wearing a dress shirt and tie. Where was he going all dressed up?

She grabbed her purse and headed out the door. She felt pathetic, but she had to know where he was sneaking off to. Was she his nighttime conquest and he had an early morning conquest somewhere else? Though where he'd get the stamina, she didn't know. They'd done it three times last night. Only once in the bed. Heat rushed through her, remembering. He'd manhandled her—flipping her this way and that, bending her over, tossing her around, carrying her, moving her as he pleased.

And she'd liked it.

She went damp. Fucking damn hell. He couldn't treat her like this. Just have his way with her and sneak off.

She headed to her car and took off down the driveway, following him at a distance. He left Eastman and headed to Clover Park, finally pulling into the parking lot of St. Joseph's Catholic church. This was his big secret meeting that he had to sneak out of bed for? She would've gone with him if he'd asked. She was Catholic, though of course he wouldn't have known that because he rarely spent any time with her just talking. She watched him get out of the car, pull his tie away from his neck, and head resolutely inside.

She waited a few minutes before following him in. He was near the front, sitting with a beautiful woman, smiling and chatting. What the hell, er, heck? She couldn't bring herself to curse in church, even in her head. She waited as people filed in. No one joined them. Just Vince and his mystery woman going to church. Omigod. Was he married? Was the carriage house just where he brought his many mistresses? No wonder it was mostly empty. His real house was somewhere else with his beautiful wife.

She sat through the service, feeling slightly queasy, but determined to find out what the *bleepity bleep* was going on. He passed by her on his way out, not noticing her in the crowd of people. She went after him and walked right up to him outside, where he was still talking to that beautiful woman. She was stunning up close. Curly hair in casual, careless layers, slender, high cheekbones. Just the kind of woman Vince would want.

Vince still hadn't noticed her. She gave him a light jab to the gut and met rock-hard abs.

"Hey!" he exclaimed. His eyes nearly popped out of his head.

"Who is she?" Sophia demanded.

"Sophia!" he exclaimed, looking all guilty. "Did you follow me?"

"Who is she, huh?" She hitched a thumb toward the woman who may or may not be Vince's wife. "Is this who you're sneaking out the door to meet?"

The woman grinned. "I'm his sister-in-law, Jasmine, and I'm married. Aren't you a ball of fire?"

Her cheeks flamed.

"Go home, Soph," Vince said. "I'll see you next weekend."

Like she was just his good-time girl when he felt like hooking up, but the rest of his life, no, thank you. *Go home.* And wasn't that always the way for her? Once she wasn't needed, get lost.

She did an about-face and hurried away as tears unexpectedly snuck up on her.

"Yo, Soph!" that moron called.

She kept going. He caught up with her and grabbed her

by the waist, lifting her right off the ground. "Jasmine said I should talk to you."

She felt like kicking him in the shin. But she really didn't want to make a scene in the church parking lot. She sighed, and he set her down and turned her to face him.

"You don't have to go home," he said. "Jasmine said that was harsh."

"Oh, thanks, Vince. Good to know."

"I just didn't want you to see me here."

"Why? It's church! What's wrong with that?"

"Nothing. It's just something I do privately."

"It's not private at all. You're sitting there with Jasmine."

"She's the godmother. We have to be active members of the church if we want to be godparents. Gabe and Zoe go to the later mass."

"Why can't I go? I'm Catholic. You just want me in your bed—" His hand clapped over her mouth.

He looked side to side. "Would you keep it down? I know people around here, and Father Munson is still skulking around, looking for sinners."

She blinked rapidly.

"Aw, don't cry, Soph." He dropped his hand. "I said I'd see you next weekend."

"Bye, Vince," she choked out.

"I'll call you."

She went back to her car and drove home. What had she expected? She knew he was clueless when it came to women. She just hadn't anticipated how much it would hurt.

Vince didn't call Sophia. He knew he wouldn't get very far that way. Instead he showed up at Sophia's door the following Friday night with a bouquet of red roses.

She pursed her lips. "You think flowers make up for the way you just toy—"

He grabbed her and kissed her. She stiffened in his arms for a moment, but then her mouth yielded. He knew how to please her. He kissed her, rough and demanding, until she sank against him.

"Where's your dad?" he asked.

"He's at my uncle's place."

"Good." Then he tossed her over his shoulder, one hand firmly on her ass, and carried her upstairs. She was hot to the touch and quiet.

Hot was good. A quiet woman, as she'd pointed out last weekend when they'd had their first fight, wasn't always good.

"Tell me what you're thinking," he said.

"I'm thinking you're a moron."

He rubbed her butt. "Which room?"

"Second one on the right."

He grinned. He might be a moron, but this moron was having his way tonight with a beautiful soon-to-be-naked woman. He stepped into her bedroom and swung her back down off his shoulder, cradled in his arms. "Hello, gorgeous."

She gave him a small smile. He swung her back and forth over the queen-size bed, she shrieked, and on the third swing he let her fly. She bounced on the mattress with a laugh. She loved when he roughhoused with her, which was good, because he loved getting physical. He was still careful with her, held back a bit so he wouldn't hurt her or crush her, but she was a helluva lot of fun. Always laughing or moaning, depending what he did.

Tonight he would make her his in a complete and total surrender. Then she would stop worrying about what he did without her. Because his early morning weekend activities didn't concern her.

And there was no way he was letting her see him in costume.

17

Sophia landed on the bed with a bounce. Vince had tossed her there like a sack of potatoes. Not exactly the romantic ending to that whole carrying-upstairs thing he'd done, which would've been a tad more romantic if she wasn't over his shoulder, but still fun. She propped up on her elbows, waiting for him to join her. Instead he grabbed her shoes and tossed them. Then he grabbed her leggings and panties by the waist and yanked them down in one swoop. He'd just walked in the door and already she was half naked. "Uh, Vince."

He pulled her up, grabbed her shirt, and yanked it over her head, tossing it to the side. "What?" he asked as he undid the bra and tossed that too.

"Did it occur to you I might like a slow seduction?" She was sitting there completely naked while he was still dressed.

He looked her up and down. "No."

Then he was on her, kissing her, his hands roaming all over her, immediately going to her hot spots, all of her erogenous zones, until she felt warm and languid and gave in. She lay back and let him do whatever he wanted. He flipped her over, shifted her hair to the side and kissed the back of her neck. He never rolled her, always flipped her back and forth. Last weekend the sudden change in position had startled her. Now she just accepted it.

His voice rumbled in her ear. "You like when I rough-house with you, don't you?"

"You mean manhandle me?"

He nipped the side of her neck, and she hissed out a breath. His tongue soothed the spot. "Manhandle," he echoed. "Yeah. You like being handled."

"I don't," she breathed, not wanting to give him any advantage.

He shed his clothes quickly. "You're a liar." And then he proved his point, turning her this way and that as easily as a doll, playing with her body, teasing, touching, handling her. By the time he had her straddling him while he kissed and stroked her with his rough hands, she was restless, moving her hips against him, needing him inside her. But he wasn't done handling her. He flipped her to her back, her side, her belly, his hands always rough and firm, making her forget herself, making her surrender.

"You're mine, Sophia," he whispered as he sat up, pulling her back with him, his arm around her waist as he leaned back against the headboard. He hauled her up into his lap. "Mine to do with as I please." Her back was against his chest, his thick erection pressing against her bottom, and she was already desperate for release. He nuzzled her neck, his fingers rolling and tugging on her nipples.

"Vince," she moaned.

He bit down on the side of her neck, holding her in place while his hand trailed down her stomach and kept going. "You're so wet for me."

She trembled as his rough callused fingers separated her folds, stroking up and down. Vince's effect on her was over-whelmingly strong. She'd never experienced anything like what he did to her. Her orgasms were shattering. And he didn't stop with just one. He kept going until she had abso-lutely nothing left.

"Please," she whispered.

"Please is good," he said. His devious fingers were slip-ping in and out of her and then slid up to do one big pinch.

She cried out, and he loosened his hold, stroking the oversensitive spot softly. "How about thank you?"

His hands moved up to pinch her nipples, and she arched her hips back, needing to feel him inside her. He slid her hand down, making her feel her own wetness. "Here, touch yourself while I get the condom."

She pulled her hand away. He pushed it back and made her hand move with his hand on top. His fingers directed hers, circling, flicking, stroking. She moaned and closed her eyes.

He released her hand. "Keep going."

She felt strange but did as he asked, enjoying her own touch more than she thought. Vince lifted her off his lap and set her in the center of the bed.

"You make me so hot when you do that," he said. She heard the rustle of the condom. "Now me."

Her eyes stayed closed, knowing Vince would arrange her into whatever position he liked. She felt his heat, his large body pressing next to her, and then he yanked her down so she was flat on her back. He pushed her hand away and spread her legs. She waited for his first hard thrust and was surprised when instead his mouth dropped down over her throbbing sex. She tried to scramble up and away from that mouth, that unforgiving mouth that pushed her way beyond release, but he just dragged her back down and his lips and teeth and tongue told her she hadn't done the right thing with that move because now he was showing her no mercy, no break, just an unrelenting suckling and licking and occasional tight tug between the teeth. She started shaking and begged him to come inside her.

"Nuh-uh," he said with another slow lick. "When you shake, that's you fighting it. I want you giving in immediately. Total surrender."

She tensed, everything inside her clenching as he lapped at her. She broke helplessly, rocking against his mouth that had started suckling her again. He kept going, driving her out of her mind, making her pant like an animal. She was drenched in sweat, in a pleasure free fall that threatened to take her under, all boundaries gone, at the absolute mercy of this man who just would not stop. The last thread of her control broke, and she followed him over peak after peak with no tensing against him, no fight at all, lost in pleasure. When he finally released her, a long feverish time later, she went limp, completely boneless and wrung out.

"Again," he said just as he thrust inside. She came immediately. She clung to him, expecting a long tumbling ride, but he drove hard and fast and exploded inside her with a hoarse groan, collapsing on top of her.

A moment later he rolled off her. He hauled her up against his side, and she needed no prompting to rest her head on his chest and wrap her arm and leg around him. His heart was pounding, which told her that while he might've worked to shake her up, he was also affected. His breathing deepened into sleep, and she felt herself drifting off. She really hoped she didn't wake to an empty bed again. Not after that. She felt shattered, raw and vulnerable, and she couldn't take the heartache.

~

Sophia woke when she felt Vince get out of bed. She opened one eye. Seven a.m. on a Saturday. "Vince?"

He froze. "Oh, hey. Didn't mean to wake you."

"What's the rush?"

"I gotta get back home. Get ready. Got a few things to do."

"You're not going to tell me?"

"I'll call you. I'll see you tonight if you're free."

"So am I just good to have around for nights? Just when you want to hook up?"

"Geez, Soph. It's too early to fight. Sometimes I gotta do stuff."

"Like what?"

He was silent. She let out a sigh. Clearly Vince didn't want her in his life. He wasn't serious about her. She should've moved back to her apartment in Brooklyn by now, but she'd stuck around because of Vince. It was time to move on. This wasn't her, just in it for the sex. She needed more than that.

He turned to go. "I'll call ya," he said over his shoulder.

Her heart ached for the man who took her out of herself, shook her up, and then left her in a cold rush.

"I'm busy tonight," she said.

He turned. "Busy with what?"

"I have to pack. I'm moving next weekend."

His face flushed with anger. She grabbed her robe and hurried into the bathroom.

Vince appeared in the doorway. "Whadda ya mean you're moving?" he boomed.

"It's time for me to go back to my real life," she said calmly. "My dad doesn't need me at the house anymore. You've got the library project running smoothly." She shrugged. "You can go now. I'm going to get ready."

"Fine," he snapped. "I'll shower here." He turned on the water and started stripping down. She took in his massive shoulders, the raw strength and power in him, and felt herself softening, going damp and needy again.

She turned away, brushing out her hair and wrapping it up in a hair band in a messy bun. His arms slipped around her from behind. "I don't want to fight." His voice, low and husky, made her insides do a delicious flip. He untied the robe and slipped it from her shoulders. Then he kissed down the side of her neck as one strong arm banded around her waist, pressing her firmly against him. "C'mon, get in the shower."

She caved. "Get a condom."

"I just want to be with you. I'll wash you."

Her knees went weak. Just when she thought she'd had him all figured out, he went and said something like that. Was there really a teddy bear hiding in that lumberjack body?

Before she had too much time to ponder that, he pulled her into the glass stall and proceeded to wash her in a gruff efficient way. It was probably the way he washed himself—

arms, armpits, chest, stomach, back, groin, legs. He was unconcerned with her sudden intake of breath over sensitive spots. He pushed her under the spray to rinse, turned her the other way, and then proceeded to wash himself in the same way. He rinsed, turned off the water, and stepped out, grabbing a towel and wrapping it around his waist. Her towel.

"Towel, please," she said. "In that closet."

He took one out, and she reached for it. He held it just out of reach.

"Gimme that!"

He pulled her out and started drying her off in his efficient way. "Where are you moving?"

She jerked as the towel flicked over her overly sensitized nipples on the way to rub down her stomach and hips. "Back to my apartment in Brooklyn."

He brought the towel between her legs, and her knees buckled. He pulled it up, making her ride it like a hammock, and an insistent throbbing returned. "Vince." She knew better than to reason with him. "Please."

He held that towel tight, making her squirm, making her want. "You didn't think to mention to me that you're moving more than an hour away? You must've been planning this for a while."

She couldn't help it. She moaned. He dropped the towel, and she stood there naked and throbbing, feeling desperate for him to stay and give her what her body now craved. She wrapped her arms around his waist. His erection pressed into her belly. "It's my home," she said.

"Your home is with me." Then he lifted her, cradled in his arms, walked back to the bedroom and tossed her on the bed. She merely opened her arms and legs to him, offering herself freely. He needed no more invitation than that. He was on her in a flash, and he took and took and took until it seemed she had always been his.

And then he left again without telling her where he was going or what he was doing. She buried her face in the pillow and screamed. But that reminded her too much of Vince and what he'd done to her, so she scrambled back out of bed and headed downstairs for some coffee. The dozen red roses were sitting on the coffee table.

She sighed. What was she supposed to do with a man like Vince?

18

———

"Omigod, no." The words were a hushed whisper as Sophia stood staring in horror that night at the sight before her—the Episcopal church annex was on fire. Most of the Clover Park Library collection, including first editions and historic town documents, had been stored there. The volunteer firefighters were battling down the blaze, dousing the building with water, and they were winning. Sophia clapped a hand over her mouth as tears threatened. Even if they got the fire out, the smoke and the water would finish the damage. She couldn't believe this. She'd gotten a call from one of the town councilmen. She'd raced to the scene, hoping there might be something salvageable. There wouldn't be.

The worst part was, she didn't know where her dad was. He wasn't at her uncle's apartment. He wasn't home. He wasn't answering his cell. The location of the fire just on the church annex smacked of sabotage. Someone who didn't want the library to be a success. She knew her dad wasn't happy about her insistence on moving forward with Marino Construction. Would he really have betrayed her like this? She didn't want to think him capable of it, but he hadn't been himself ever since her mom left. She hated that she even thought it.

She wanted to call Vince and tell him about this horrible

turn of events, but she felt weird. Sure, they'd had two weekends of crazy-good sex, but they'd left things unsettled.

The last of the flames died down, and she pulled out her cell. She was being ridiculous. This was Vince's project too. Of course he should know. Maybe it was accidental. She was being paranoid just because she felt such a personal connection to what they'd lost. Her gut churned. Hundred-year-old documents. Some even older. She should've known better. She should've put them in a fireproof safe. Clover Park's history was in her hands and now it was gone.

Vince answered right away. "Hey, Sophia." That deep, melodic voice reassured her somehow. So strong and steady.

"Hi," she said.

"Miss me already?"

She kinda did, actually, even though she'd spent nearly twenty-four hours pressed against his solid body. "There was a fire. The church annex—"

"Shit. Are you okay? Where are you?"

"I'm okay. I'm at the church. The fire is out."

"Did we lose all those books?"

He said *we*. He really did see it as their project. Her dad had been all wrong about Vince. He kept warning her that the Marinos would take over, push them out, but Vince hadn't been like that at all.

"Sophia, talk to me! Forget it. I'll be right there."

"No! I'm going home. It's like a car crash. I can't seem to look away." She swallowed over the lump in her throat. "It's all my fault."

"This is not your fault. I'm heading to your place. Hang tight." He hung up.

She watched for a few more moments, the lights of the fire trucks swirling through the dark, the shouts of the men. Slowly, she turned and headed home.

By the time Vince got there, Sophia had had a chance to calm down. She still felt incredibly guilty for not doing more to preserve those historic documents, but the initial shock had worn off. She opened the door, and Vince swooped in, wrapping his arms around her and lifting her off the ground in his enthusiasm.

"Vince." She laughed. "I'm okay."

He set her down and studied her. "You smell like smoke, and you sounded terrible on the phone. What happened?"

"Come in." She gestured to the sofa and headed over to it.

"How bad is the damage over there?"

"The roof collapsed. Half the walls are gone. The other half are charred. They were lucky to contain it. The church has one wall with damage, but the rest is still standing." She leaned forward and dropped her head in her hands. "There's no way anything left in there is salvageable. Not after the flames and the smoke and all that water. I should've moved the historic documents to a safe location. Why didn't I? Now we'll have this historic building with nothing historic left to put in it."

His large warm hand rubbed her back. "We still have some things. That fireplace, right? The original windows. You said you were getting the chandelier back from the town hall attic. Maybe they have some old papers stored there too. That place is wall-to-wall file cabinets."

That hadn't occurred to her. "Maybe."

He stroked her hair. "It wasn't your fault."

She straightened. "I know I didn't set the fire, but I should've done more. I know about archival storage. I just…I guess I wasn't thinking. The annex was just supposed to be a short-term solution."

"You were distracted by working with a sexy beast."

She reluctantly smiled. "Oh, Vince."

"Do they know what caused the fire?"

"No, but the pastor wasn't home. He lives in the house next to the church. Nobody saw anything until the smoke." She shook her head. "There was so much smoke." All those old papers ruined.

"I want to talk to the fire department. See if it was an accident or arson."

She stiffened at the mention of arson. She was a little worried her dad had been involved. He'd been really worked up about working with the Marinos, and he'd been doing crazy things lately. It wasn't just the alpaca farm. He'd been calling the home phone from his cell *while he was at home*, even though he didn't like to use his cell, just to listen to her mom on the voicemail. He'd even been reading self-help books like *The Nitwit's Guide to Saving a Marriage* and *Supercoupling for Super Couples*. Not to mention the fact that he slept with her mom's winter coat under his pillow. (She'd taken her clothes with her, but didn't need the coat in Florida.) The last thing they needed was an investigation into her dad after he'd taken all that money from the company. Even if he was innocent, an investigation would destroy his reputation. No one would want to work with him.

"I'm sure it wasn't deliberate," she said.

"Could've been someone who wanted to sabotage the project," Vince said.

"No."

"Or maybe someone that didn't like the project," he said.

Her temper flared. "You mean my dad!" It was fine for her to think it. An entirely different thing for Vince to throw stones at her dad.

"Calm down," he said as his hand slid into her hair, cupping the back of her neck. "It could've been anyone."

"I don't like what you're implying," she said right before he squeezed the back of her neck, easing some of the tension there. She had no willpower when it came to those hands.

"You're so tense."

"I'm upset! The fire—"

Next thing she knew she was face down on the sofa. He'd flipped her there in one quick move, and she landed stretched out across the length of the sofa. "Vince!" she protested.

But then those strong hands were massaging her shoulders and working their way down her back, and she surrendered to the most delicious massage of her life.

By Tuesday, the investigators had concluded arson. Sophia had spoken with the police, cleared her name, but she'd been forced to admit she didn't know where her dad was when no one could get in touch with him for questioning. She hadn't been allowed in the annex to inspect the collection because it was still under investigation, but it was clear from her view through the window that nothing was left. She'd gone to the town hall and discovered, thankfully, that they stored historic tax and real estate records there. What had been lost were volumes of surveys, original maps, and several histories that had been written about the town going back to 1920. Also, some first editions of local authors, including one by Mark Twain. She felt sick about the whole thing.

After several days of being a nervous wreck, waiting at home for her dad to return, and praying that he hadn't been involved, she finally gave up. He wasn't coming home. He was completely unreachable, and she hated that it implied guilt, hated thinking her own father would sabotage the project she'd worked so hard on to save their family business. If it was true, this was one mess that even she couldn't make right.

Her boss was on her back about coming back to the city, so she finally decided on Friday to move back to her old brownstone apartment in Brooklyn. Their office was there and most of their consulting jobs were in the city. She'd leave the Clover Park Library project in Vince's capable hands until she was needed when the historic designation application came back. It pained her to think of all Clover Park had lost on account of her and her family. This was the best choice for everyone.

It was the day before Halloween, and she had plans to meet up with friends at a costume party. It almost felt normal. She wouldn't be seeing Vince tonight, which was fine. They had their own lives. He'd said he was going out tonight for drinks with the guys and Brooklyn was too damn far a commute on a Friday night. He wasn't happy with her move, but she wasn't sure what exactly he'd expected from her. Yes, they'd had amazing sex and three official dates (she wouldn't count the times they went straight to bed as dates), but it wasn't like she was going to move in with him. And she couldn't stay at her parents' house, a frazzled mess waiting for her dad to return home.

She wore a kitty-cat costume with a black body suit, a headband with kitty ears, and a tail. Her roommate, Roger, wore a black tux with a sign taped to his front that read *I'm sorry*. He was a formal apology. She couldn't help but smile every time she saw him. The bell rang shrilly.

She answered the door, and her hand went to her throat. Vince was standing there in a Marino and Sons construction shirt under a brown leather jacket, looking all kinds of sexy. It was shocking the instant arousal just seeing him produced—heart pounding, hot all over, damp between the legs. She'd never felt like that just from looking at someone.

"What are you doing here?" she asked. "I thought you were getting a drink with the guys tonight."

"I changed my mind." He stepped inside, wrapped an arm around her waist and pulled her with him into the apartment before claiming her mouth. The door slammed shut behind him. His lips were hard and demanding, his tongue thrust deep, and she sank against him, a puddle of need.

Roger cleared his throat. Vince pulled back, glowered at Roger, and turned back to her. "Who the hell is that?"

"He's my roommate. Vince, this is Roger." Roger was a very sweet website designer with shaggy dirty blond hair, black-rimmed glasses, and a huge collection of bowties. He had a girlfriend in Canada. At least he said he did. Sophia had never met the woman.

Roger extended his hand. "Nice to meet you."

Vince stared at the offered hand. "You have a guy roommate!" he boomed.

Sophia grimaced. Roger cringed. "Just friends," Roger quickly said.

"I'm her boyfriend," Vince said, pumping Roger's hand.

"Got it," Roger said, discreetly shaking his hand out after Vince released it. He turned to her. "Are you still going to the party or..."

"Of course," Sophia said. "I'm sure Evelyn won't mind if I

bring a guest. Just a minute." She backed a few steps away to text Evelyn just to be sure and heard Vince saying he was in construction.

Roger laughed a little too hard. "I guess someone has to be. I can't even put together a shelf. I'm in website design."

"Guess someone has to be," Vince said.

"You wear a hard hat to work?" Roger asked. "Do you sit on a girder and eat from a lunchbox?"

Sophia cringed and glanced up to see Roger elbow Vince, who did a quick blocking move that pushed Roger's arm away.

Roger went on. "Ever bury someone in the concrete?"

"I wear a hard hat when I need to," Vince said. "You watch a lot of TV? Cuz you sound like all you know is some stereotype about construction workers. And just because I'm Italian doesn't mean I'm Mafia."

"No, no, of course not," Roger said.

"Yo, Soph!" Vince called. She winced. It really made him sound coarse and ill-mannered to call her that way. "You believe this guy?"

Her cell chimed back with a text. Evelyn was fine with her bringing a guest. She looked at Vince in his jeans and long-sleeve Marino Construction shirt. She should get him a costume. Maybe Roger had something.

"Soph?" Vince asked. The uncertainty in his usually confident voice pulled at her.

She hurried over. "Evelyn says it's okay. And Roger, behave yourself. We law-abiding Italians take offense to Mafia references."

"Sorry," Roger said.

Vince hauled her against his side and kissed the top of her head. She felt simultaneously manhandled and the gentlest of touches with that kiss. And wasn't that just Vince in a nutshell? Gruff and rough and yet surprisingly gentle at times.

She looked up at him. "It's a costume party. You want to see if Roger has something—"

"I've got those funny glasses with the nose and mustache

from when I was an identity thief," Roger offered. The costume was just the glasses and a hoodie covered with *Hello, my name is* stickers. Roger had a great sense of humor.

"Nah," Vince said. "I don't need a costume."

"Let me get the wine and we can go," Sophia said. She snagged the bottle, and they made the short walk to Evelyn's while Sophia scrambled to find conversation that both Vince and Roger could join in. Roger wanted to fill her in on the latest gossip among their friends—who had hooked up with who, who had rekindled old flames—while Vince wanted to fill her in on the latest with construction on the library project. They talked over each other, each vying for her attention.

"Please!" she said. "I can only listen to one of you at a time."

"Sorry, Vince," Roger said. "I have a lot to catch Sophia up on. She hasn't been around much the last few months."

"She's been with me," Vince said, dropping his arm over her shoulders.

Roger was undeterred by Vince's menacing tone and went on and on about Betsy getting back with Bob, and Tilly and her unending on-again, off-again relationship with Holden.

They made it to the party. She kissed Evelyn on the cheek, handed over the wine, and introduced Vince.

"H-hi," Evelyn said before turning bright red.

"Hello," Vince said in his deep, melodic voice. "Thank you for having me."

Oh, thank goodness, his manners were back. Vince surprised her, charming all of her girl friends, who were all reduced to blushing and stammering. Everyone exclaimed over his construction worker "costume" and he didn't correct them, just let them fawn all over him. Evelyn even squeezed his bicep. Yes, he was gorgeous, but she hadn't thought her intellectual friends would be reduced to stammering and simpering in his presence. He gave her a wink and a smile. The men on the other hand…Vince was gruff and aggressive, making sure they all knew he was her boyfriend.

The talk turned to politics, her friends were all liberals, but liked to argue both sides of every issue for sport. Vince ignored the talk, instead standing at her side, his hand rubbing up and down her back, occasionally shifting to run up and down her side, keeping her hot and bothered. She couldn't tell if he was having a good time or not. He'd gotten so quiet. After an hour or so, Evelyn called for a game of charades.

"When can we get out of here?" Vince whispered in her ear.

"You're not having a good time?"

He wrapped one arm around her waist, resting his hand on her hip. "This isn't my scene."

"It's my scene."

He hauled her against his side. "I want you."

"You can have me later."

His hand shifted, his fingers spreading wide across her belly, setting off tingles of sensation to all of her favorite parts. "I want you now."

"Come on over, guys!" Evelyn caroled.

Sophia held up a finger. "Just a minute."

Vince turned her to face him, his deep brown eyes burning into hers. "Soph," he said in a low, husky voice, "I held up my end. I showed you fisting the sheets. Now it's your turn."

She throbbed. Her turn? With that delicious body? To do as she pleased? He never let her take control. He nodded at her, seeming to read her mind.

She turned and looked at Evelyn, who smiled and waved them over. Vince's hand connected with her ass and squeezed, hot and possessive.

"We're going to pass," Sophia squeaked. She stepped away from him. "Vince has to get back home soon."

"It's Friday night," Evelyn said. "Come on. Have a little fun."

But Vince was already pulling her from the room. "Bye," she called. "Thank you!"

"Bye," Vince boomed.

19

———

Sophia was thoroughly enjoying torturing Vince with hot kisses and little nibbles all over that delicious muscular body. He was naked, lying on his back in her bed with his hands laced behind his head as she insisted. He looked like an honest-to-God centerfold, and he was hers to play with all night long. She'd already explored his neck and delicious chest with a brief stop to revel in those massive biceps. By the time she licked his happy trail, he was breathing hard. He jerked as she got closer to her target. Then she took him in her mouth, and he hissed out a breath. She pulled back, ran her tongue up and down his length, and then took him in deep. He groaned, and his hand gripped her hair, keeping her on him. A few more long suctioning strokes, and he jackknifed up, flipped her on her back, and settled between her legs.

"Vince, you said it was my turn."

He kissed her gently and pulled back to look in her eyes. "You had your turn, dream girl. You're too good at that."

She smiled. "I am?"

"Yes, and I don't want to know why."

"I want more of my turn," she pouted.

He nipped her lower lip. "I never let someone else take charge in bed. You're the first."

"Then let me do more."

He didn't deny her, but he didn't let her up either. Instead he reached for a condom and rolled it on. Then he lifted her hips at just the right angle and slid deep. She moaned, and he stilled. He stroked her hair back from her face. "I love you, Soph."

Her eyes widened. "You do?"

One corner of his mouth lifted. "Is that so hard to believe?"

"No, I don't—" Her reply was cut off with a kiss and then there was no more conversation as her body responded to him as he demanded at his pace for as long as he pleased.

Vince pulled Sophia close and held her for a long time. He'd never experienced the intensity of what he had with Sophia in bed. He loved her, and though it pained him that she hadn't returned the words, he didn't regret saying them for the first time ever. It felt good to have someone to love.

Her hand was rubbing his chest absentmindedly. "Vince, I'm worried."

He pulled her tighter against him, ready to help with whatever it was. "Worried about what?"

She didn't say anything for a long moment. He waited.

"I-I can't get in touch with my dad," she finally said. "It's been a week and I don't know where he is." She lifted her head, her eyes full of pain and worry, and Vince wanted nothing more than to take all that pain and worry away. "What if something happened to him? It's not like him to be out of touch so long."

"Shh." He pressed her head down to his chest. "I'm sure he's fine. He's a grown man. Tough like a pit bull, right?"

She let out a shaky breath.

"Go to sleep," he said.

"I can't. I haven't slept well ever since the fire." She lifted her head again and the look of painful conflict on her face was more than he could take. He knew if it was her dad behind the fire, she'd be devastated. He'd protect her from that at all costs.

The hard truth was—her dad was the only one with a strong motive. He didn't want them working together, didn't like Vince hanging around his daughter, and had threatened to take over the project. Not only that, he had no alibi for the day of the fire and, most damning, he'd gone into hiding.

If Sophia's dad showed up at the groundbreaking ceremony on Monday, as Vince suspected he would, being the publicity whore he was, he planned on talking to him about the arson and how to make this problem go away. Because if the police found out, both companies would be sunk.

He flipped her onto her back in one quick move. "I'm gonna wear you out, Soph. And then you'll sleep."

"Vince! Not everything can be fixed—"

He claimed her mouth, stroked her hard and firm, and she quieted, heating against him, opening to him. She was his to love, to protect, and, yes, to fix any problems she brought to him by any means necessary.

The glow from Vince's declaration of love and long night of tender loving wore off the next morning when he got up early and left the bed. Sophia squeezed her eyes shut tight over the sting of tears. How could he say he loved her and yet never let her in? Maybe he didn't really love her. Maybe it just slipped out in the throes of passion.

She sat up and pulled the sheet up to her neck, watching him pull on his jeans. "Don't let the door hit you on the way out."

He let out a noisy sigh and turned. "Are you mad?"

"No."

"You sound mad."

She battled between mad and trying to be understanding about his general cluelessness when it came to women. Did she have to spell it out? You don't just hook up and then leave. She opened her mouth to tell him just that when he interrupted.

"Look, I'm new to all this relationship stuff, so why don't you save us both some time and tell me what you're mad about."

"We have a relationship?"

"We've been dating four weeks!" he roared.

"Don't yell at me!"

"I said I love you." He jammed his hands on his hips. "That's a relationship. What would you call it?"

He said it again. Out of bed. Her heart squeezed. "A relationship."

"Thank you." He sat next to her on the bed, wearing only jeans. She forced herself not to touch because that would be the end of any meaningful conversation. "Now tell me why you're mad."

"It's just the way you race out of bed after we hook up."

"I told you I gotta be someplace."

She sighed. "Last time you rushed off it was church. Let me guess, on Saturdays you visit sick children at the hospital."

The tips of his ears reddened.

"Omigod, you do! Why are you hiding good things from me? Are you trying to preserve some player rep?"

He turned away and spoke to the wall. "I don't want you to see me in costume."

"There's a costume? What kind of costume?"

He stood. "It doesn't matter. There, now I told you, so you can stop freaking out every time I gotta do something."

"Is it Big Bird?"

He sputtered. "No, it's not Big Bird!"

"Well, you're tall enough. What is it?"

He mumbled something she couldn't quite catch. She stood and wrapped her arms around his waist. "Say that again."

His hands started roaming along her bare back. "A porcupine."

"A porcupine?" She bit back a laugh.

"You're laughing at me." He peeled her off him and stepped away.

"I'm not! I was just surprised." She threw herself in his arms again. "Why a porcupine?"

He told her about the picture book series his stepmom created about him and his brothers—the Huddles and Cuddles. She suddenly remembered the picture books that were the only books on the bookcase at his place. Vince explained there were hedgehogs (his stepbrothers) and porcupines (him, Nico, and Angel) who battled and then worked out their differences. Apparently he was the leader of the porcupines.

"I want to see the costume," she said.

"No."

"This is what people in relationships do," she said with a straight face. "They see each other in costume. You saw me as a kitty cat. I'm coming with you."

He stepped away, but she clung to him, not letting him escape. He palmed her ass and pressed her against him. "Soph, I look ridiculous. You're not going to want to sleep with me after you see me like this."

She smiled up at him. "Actually, I'll want you even more."

He smiled uncertainly. "Yeah?"

"Yup."

He ground her against him. "How much more?"

"Like anything you want more."

His gaze heated. "Anything?"

She nodded. The truth was he owned her in that bed, and now knowing what he really did with his weekend mornings, she just fell heart thumping, head-over-heels, can't-even-think-straight in love.

He looked painfully conflicted. She wrapped her arms around his neck and kissed him.

He pulled back. "You handling me, Soph?"

"Damn right. I learned from the best. Ah!" He'd grabbed her and turned her upside down. "Vince! Put me down!"

"If you laugh at me in that costume, you will pay. I will show no mercy."

He'd shown mercy before? Even upside down, he turned her on. "I won't laugh," she promised.

He set her back on the ground. She looked at his disgruntled expression, love surging through her heart. "I love you, Vince."

He sucked in an audible breath. "When you didn't say it before…" He grabbed her and hauled her up against him. "I love you too."

She spoke into his chest where she was comfortably nestled. "Tell me how this whole porcupine thing got started."

He sighed and spoke over her shoulder, still holding her tight. "One of my guys on crew, his boy Jaden was sick. Leukemia. I started visiting him at the hospital. I didn't know what to say to the kid. I mean, it sucks, you know? So I read him the Huddles and Cuddles books that I loved as a kid. Then more kids wanted to hear the stories. One of the nurses, Emily, made me a costume."

She pulled back to look at him. "Does it have quills?"

He pushed her back against his chest, so she couldn't see his face. His voice rumbled in his chest. "Yes." She stayed utterly still, hoping he'd continue to talk. "The kids went bananas. It was good for a while, you know? Jaden was getting a kick out of it. But he was getting worse, weaker." He went quiet, and she held her breath. "He…died last summer." His voice came out choked.

She pulled back to look in his eyes shiny with unshed tears. "I'm so sorry."

He blinked and rubbed one eye with a fist. "I stopped going. Emily called me, said the kids missed me and it made things worse to lose Jaden and me. I've been going ever since."

"I think my ovaries just exploded."

He cocked his head. "What?"

"That is beautiful. Now why were you hiding that from me all this time?"

"I look like an idiot in that outfit."

"I'm coming with you."

"No."

She held his face in her hands. "I love you. All the parts. The sexy parts. The idiot parts. I want it all." His large hand covered one of hers. "Give me it all," she demanded.

His eyes watered. "Whatcha doing to me, Soph?"

"I'm loving you."

He kissed her, backing her up until her knees hit the back of the bed, then with one little push he had her on her back. He smiled wickedly. "You owe me *anything*."

"That was after I went with you to the hosp—" The words died in her throat as Vince slowly undid his zipper. She swallowed as his jeans and briefs hit the floor, then he joined her, and the rest was fingers-fisting-in-the-sheets oblivion.

20

———

Vince sighed and looked to the ceiling where he stood at the nurses' station in the pediatric hematology-oncology ward of Eastman Hospital. The women were *oohing* and *aahhing* over his costume, giggling about how cute he was. This *always* happened. And he could tell Sophia was trying not to laugh.

This was exactly why he got his part of the deal upfront from Sophia. He knew she would think he looked ridiculous. He'd be lucky to ever get her naked again. And even if he did, she'd always be picturing him like this—bright red T-shirt with a felt C sewn on the front, a red eye mask, a gray knit cap with gray yarn that stuck up every which way for quills, and a blue cape. He refused to wear tights.

"Do you have a special name?" Sophia asked, fighting back a smile.

Emily, the nurse who made him the costume, grinned and handed him the goody bag. "He's Captain Cuddle. I put some spider rings in there for Halloween."

He nodded. Today was Halloween, and the nurses had decorated for it, but none of the kids in the hematology-oncology ward would be trick-or-treating. There were about ten to twenty kids usually because Eastman had a specialty team for kids with cancer that drew people from all over the tri-state area.

"The captain part was not my idea," Vince mumbled. "The kids just started calling me that."

"Can I be co-captain?" Sophia asked with a grin, eyes dancing with amusement.

"There's no such thing," he muttered. "I have to get started before visiting hours end." He grabbed the stack of Huddle Cuddle books and headed resolutely into the ward. He always stopped at the sickest kids rooms first because they tired out quickly. Sophia trailed behind him.

"Knock, knock," he boomed.

"Who's there?" Olivia said with a giggle. She had leukemia too like Jaden. They'd been friends. She was skinny, had lost her hair, and was nine.

He bounded into the room.

"Captain Cuddle!" she exclaimed.

"In the flesh. I brought my friend Sophia today."

Sophia smiled and waved, but stayed in the background.

"This is Candace," Olivia said, pointing to a new girl in the other bed with blond hair in pigtails. "She has leukemia too. Newly diagnosed." Sometimes Olivia sounded much older than her years. Probably from spending so much time with adults.

"Hi, Candace," he said. "Have you heard of the Huddle Cuddle books? My mom wrote them."

He held them up. Candace shook her head.

"Read *The Huddle Cuddle Water Balloon Fight*," Olivia said. "That always sounds like fun. I never did that before."

Vince had many times. His stepmom pulled most of her stories from real life. He'd never thought his childhood anything special, but when he got to know some of the kids here and what their daily life was like, full of tests and treatments and surgeries, he'd realized his childhood was pretty idyllic.

He pulled the book from the pile and set the others on a small table along with the goody bag. He always saved the goodies for the end, so they'd have something fun to play with while he moved to the next room. He held up the cover for both of them to see; then he turned the book so he could read the story and they could still see the pictures. His stepmom's artwork was incredible—detailed, realistic, but also a bit magical. He didn't know what it was, but the pictures drew you in and made you feel like you could live in this enchanted forest where hedgehogs and porcupines could speak and play.

"The leader of the Huddles wasn't happy that day," he began. He smiled to himself, checking out the leader of the Huddles that he knew was based on his brother Gabe. Olivia clapped. "It seemed he'd been hit quite unexpectedly on his way to his favorite swing with a water balloon. Splat!"

The girls giggled. He glanced at Sophia, who looked very serious. He returned to the story and acted out a bit of the water balloon fight to keep things interesting. When he finished, Olivia started chanting, "More, more, more!"

"Two more and then I have to go to the next room. You know the drill. And since Candace is new here, I'm going to read *The Huddle Cuddle School Smashup*." That was based on when he and his brothers had started going to Clover Park schools after their dad married their stepmom. "Sucks to be the new kid, right?"

Olivia giggled. "You said a bad word."

He did? "Which one?"

"Sucks!"

"Oh. That's not really bad. Okay, *no fun* to be the new kid." He read that one too and added some gory bloody detail to a playground brawl that his stepmom hadn't included, but he thought made it more exciting. He finished with the last book and both girls begged him to stay.

"Ladies, I'll be back next weekend. You get a parting gift." He opened the goody bag. The gifts were something he'd wanted to do, but he didn't know what kids would like, so he'd worked out a deal with Emily where he gave her money every Saturday and she filled it with little toys and trinkets she thought the kids would like. He eyed the girls. "You like bracelets or spider rings?"

"Bracelets!" the girls chorused.

He pulled out some rubber bracelets that had smiley faces on them and flowers. A few had words like Strength and Courage and Hope. He got a lump in his throat. These kids had all three.

He stopped in front of Candace. "Pick one."

She spent a long time looking at each one. "I'll take the pink one with flowers," she said in a whispery soft voice. "Thank you."

He handed it over and turned to Olivia. "Let me guess, purple." That was her favorite color. She had purple every-thing—pajamas, a special blankie, even her teddy bear wore a purple dress.

She nodded and held out her hand. The pale flesh of her inner arm had scars from all of the needle pricks she'd received. He gave her the bracelet, and she unexpectedly grabbed him around the middle and hugged him. "Thank you, Captain Cuddle."

He patted her shoulder awkwardly. "You're welcome, Awesome Olivia." The girl clung to him. "Hey, now, you okay?"

She looked up at him with big puppy eyes. "You're the best part of Saturday and it's over."

"All right, you little con artist, you win with those puppy eyes. Two more stories and then that's it."

She grinned and sat back in bed, waiting. This was by far the most difficult part of this gig. The kids were just stuck here, mostly alone in their beds, and desperate for something fun in their lives. She drifted to sleep before he'd even finished the next story. He made an exaggerated shushing motion to Candace and left.

He finished up his visit three hours later. He never wanted to shortchange any of them. If they really wanted him to stay, he did. As long as he'd still have time to get to the others before visiting hours ended.

He headed back to the nurses' station to pay Emily for the goody bag stuff and say goodbye. Sophia walked at his side, looking serious. He elbowed her. "Tough gig, huh?"

"I don't know how you do it," she said.

He frowned. He'd meant it was a tough gig for the kids. "It's easy for me. I'm just reading picture books and handing out stuff. It's the kids who've got it tough." He'd grown up with a sick mom. It didn't faze him.

She took his arm and held it as they walked. "Thank you for letting me see you like this. It was beautiful."

"Even the porcupine hat?"

She smiled. "Especially the porcupine hat."

To Vince's surprise, Sophia was still hot for him that night. They went back to her place because she'd wanted to take him to her favorite restaurant in Brooklyn for dinner. Her roommate was gone for the weekend, visiting his girlfriend in Canada. He'd really thought the costume would've made her giggly every time she clapped eyes on him. He knew he'd have a hard time forgetting it if she walked around with some weird hat and cape.

She was unexpectedly aggressive in bed, and they'd had a crazy tangle in the sheets because he was always aggressive. She was kind of a perfect match for him. For the first time he saw the appeal of being tied down to one woman.

The tied-down-to-one-woman idea became less appealing the next morning when Sophia was all up in his business just because he got out of bed early. He had to drive more than an hour to go home and get ready for his mandatory godfather church duty. It wasn't like he was skulking on his cuddle duty either. Last night he'd held her for way more than seven minutes.

She snagged his arm where he sat on the edge of the bed about to make a break for it. "Now what's the deal with church?" she asked. "Why can't I go with you?"

He groaned and peeled her off his arm. She leaped on his back, and he nearly fell forward at the unexpected move. She wrapped her arms and legs around him like a damn monkey. He could easily flip her over his shoulder or bring her around to his front, but she was naked and felt damn good back there. Besides it was easier to talk when he didn't have to look at those deep brown eyes that he knew would be looking at him with pity. "It's not a big deal, Soph."

She spoke in a husky voice right into his ear. "You a sinner?"

Damn, he wanted her again. But he was going to be late if he didn't get going. There could be bridge traffic. He looked at her over his shoulder. "You know I am."

"I'm going with you."

"No."

"I'll go with you just like this," she threatened. "Naked woman on your back. Is that what you want?"

He chuckled. Wouldn't that be a sight for Father Munson? "I don't want you to see me there."

"Why? I saw you as a porcupine. Why can't I see you in a shirt and tie?"

He really didn't want to have this conversation. He was about to stand and flip her over his shoulder when she scooted around to his front, wrapping that delicious body around his naked one, pressing up close enough to make his cock pulse against her.

"How about naked woman on your front in church?" she asked with a cheeky grin. "Does that work better for you?"

He pushed her hair back where it had fallen in her face, all tousled like she'd had a good roll in the hay. Which she had. "You're a piece of work."

"I know." Then she started kissing his neck, her hot mouth licking and nibbling away. "Tell me the problem, and I'll fix it."

"The problem is I want to screw your brains out, but I have to get back before I miss Mass and disqualify myself as godfather."

She met his eyes. "I saw you last week at church. How come Jasmine gets to sit with you and I can't?"

"Don't worry about her. She's married and practically family. Her sister married my brother."

"I'm not worried." She kissed him on the mouth, and he

welcomed the distraction. He returned the kiss in his usual aggressive way, hoping she'd forget all about this conversation. When he finally let her up for air, she looked dazed, and her eyes were hazy with lust. He picked her up and set her back on the bed.

"I'll call you," he said.

She rolled out of bed and started getting dressed. "I'm coming with you."

"Soph."

"It's a free country. I can go to whatever church I feel like. If I happen to want to go to your church when you're there, I can go."

"Did I say you were my dream girl?" he thundered. "More like a nightmare."

She gave him a small smile. "I love you too."

That hit him right in the gut. "M-me too." He swallowed, not used to this love stuff. "Love you, I mean."

"Get dressed," she ordered. "We don't want to be late."

He sighed and jammed a hand in his hair. "I can't take communion, okay?"

She stopped, sweater in hand, just standing there in her pink bra and panties, looking like his wet dream. It was a good distraction from the way his stomach was doing a slow churn over what she was pushing him to admit.

"Why not?" she asked.

"Because I haven't been to confession since I was nine years old." You had to go to regular confession to take communion. And he had to be all fessed up by the baptism, where taking communion was mandatory. He wasn't at all sure he'd make it there by February when the baptism was scheduled.

She pulled the sweater on. "So go to confession."

He shook his head. "No amount of Hail Marys can make up for what I've done."

Her brows lowered and a crinkle appeared in her forehead. "What did you do? It can't be that bad."

He stared at a point just over her shoulder and it all came out in a painful rush. "I broke the commandment. I didn't honor my mother. I haven't been to her grave to pay my respects since the funeral. I wished for a new mom while she was sick." His throat closed up, and he took a deep breath. "I can't even remember her healthy. When I got my stepmom, I thanked God for the new mom and started calling her mom. I was mad at my sick mom for being a crappy mom." He sucked in a breath and waited to hear how horrible he really was in her eyes.

"You were just a kid," she said.

His gaze snapped to hers. "Well, now I'm thirty-four, and I still haven't visited her."

She pulled on a skirt. "We'll go."

"I can't." He turned away and yanked on his briefs and jeans.

"I'll go with you."

"Soph, no. This is why I didn't want to tell you all this. I'm never going." He pulled on his shirt and headed down the hallway to the bathroom to wash up. Sophia joined him, brushing her teeth next to him at the sink.

She spit, rinsed, and looked at him in the mirror. "If you let me go with you to church today, I'll stay at your place all week. Naked. Helluva commute back to the city in the mornings, but I'll do it."

He raised a brow. Naked at his place sounded really good. He could have her as much as he wanted and not have to wait for the weekend. What a negotiator.

He finished brushing and turned to her. "You handling me?"

She put a hand on her hip. "That's right."

"You got five minutes to pack, and then I'm tossing you over my shoulder, bag or no bag."

Her eyes lit up.

"You like that idea, don't you?" he asked, stalking her right out of the bathroom and into the bedroom.

"N-no."

He grinned and tossed her over his shoulder. She squealed. He carried her to the full-length mirror hanging on the back of the door. "Look at you, monkey girl. You are so turned on right now."

"Am not."

He slid his hand between her legs, hot and wet. She moaned. Served her right for being all up in his business. She could just stay like that all through church, the little minx.

He set her down. "Go pack a bag, and I'll handle you more at my place."

"Will you show me your secret tower?" She was obsessed with the tower of the carriage house, which he hadn't let her go in because it wasn't safe.

"I've got a tower for you."

"I mean it."

He let out a noisy sigh of exasperation. "It's not a secret tower. I'm all out of secrets with you." Except for the one about your dad committing arson. He pushed that thought aside. He'd handle it before she knew a thing.

"Can I see it?"

"I told you it's not safe. The floorboards have some rot. I haven't gotten to it yet."

"I'll be careful." She grabbed a brush off the dresser and brushed out her long silky brown hair. So beautiful.

He crossed to her, took the brush and did it for her. He stroked her hair with his hand after he brushed it, reveling in the silky feel.

"When will it be safe?" she asked.

This woman never gave up. She was as much a pit bull as her father.

"When I get some free time," he said. "I've been busy with work and keeping you in line." He swatted her ass.

"And being a good Catholic porcupine," she teased.

He jabbed a warning finger in her face. "Don't you tell. I'll make you pay big time." The only person who knew he was Captain Cuddle was Jared because he worked at the hospital. Vince had run into him unexpectedly one time in the parking lot and Jared had insisted on following him in to watch for a bit. Vince had threatened him with castration if he ever spoke a word about it. He hadn't.

Sophia grinned, seeming unconcerned with his threats. "I won't…as long as you stay on my good side."

What a woman. Standing up to him, threatening him right back. Most people, man or woman, were intimidated by his size and his tough talk. He hauled her against him. "I want you so bad right now."

She laughed. "I know."

21

Sophia sat next to Vince at church. They'd made it to the last service, so they missed seeing Jasmine, who went to the earlier one. Vince grew increasingly tense as it got closer to communion time. And when people finally started to go up for communion, herself included, he sat with his hands folded and head bowed. It slayed her. He had such a big heart—she could see that clear as day now—yet he was riddled with guilt because of some misguided sense of right and wrong. He'd been a kid when his mom died. Of course he'd wished for things to be different.

She returned to her seat and took his hand. She gave him a small smile that he didn't return. She had to fix this. He couldn't go to church, week after week, feeling terrible about himself. He'd done nothing wrong, and she was sure that a talk with the priest would clear things up. After church, she took Vince's hand and led him to the line of people outside waiting to greet the priest. They were third in line.

"Let's go," Vince said, pulling her hand.

"Just a minute. I want to say hello." She raised a hand and waved at the priest, making sure he knew she and Vince were waiting. Vince stopped pulling at her and stood there still as a statue.

Finally, it was their turn.

"Hello, Father," Vince said. "My friend Sophia wanted to meet you. Sophia, this is Father Munson."

She gave Vince a second look. He didn't even want to call her his girlfriend to the priest? Father Munson shook her hand warmly. "Wonderful to meet you. I hope you enjoyed the sermon."

The sermon had been about All Saints' Day, which was what had been celebrated before Halloween. "Absolutely," she said. "Father, can I ask you a personal question?"

"Of course. Should we step inside?"

She nodded. The priest greeted a few more people on his way back into the now empty church, and they followed in his wake.

"What is it, my dear?" Father Munson asked.

"Does honoring your deceased mother or father require visiting their grave, or is it enough to hold them in your heart?" Sophia asked.

Vince sucked in an audible breath.

"Holding them in your heart is all that's required," the priest said with a sympathetic look to Vince. "They know."

"Thank you," Sophia said. "I feel much better now."

"Anytime."

"Thank you, Father," Vince said. "I'll see you next Sunday."

And then they were out the door, Vince pulling her down the long sidewalk and through the parking lot at an alarming speed. She could barely catch her breath. Finally they stopped at his car. He slammed his hands on his hips and glowered down at her. "You crossed the line, Soph."

She put her hands on her hips, imitating his stance. "You're getting communion next week."

"I didn't confess anything!" he barked.

"You don't have anything to confess! You didn't break any commandment."

He scowled some more. She rubbed his arm. "You can thank me later," she said.

He shook his head and shot her a dark look. "I would

thank you, but I'm too busy coming up with ways to get my revenge." He frowned. "I still have to go to confession."

"So confess like any other good Catholic. Leave out the juicy bits, say a few Hail Marys, and move on."

Vince looked to the sky. Then he turned back to her. "Get in." He opened the car door, and she slid in.

He got in the driver's side, started the car, and headed out. "You can't just get up in my business and fix stuff."

"So you admit I fixed the problem."

He blew out a breath. "Just don't—"

"Do you feel better about going to church?"

"That doesn't mean—"

"Yes or no?"

He let out a noisy breath. "Yes."

"Then it seems I did the right thing."

He scowled. "You're trying to handle me again."

"I was helping," she insisted. "Because I love you."

He shook a finger at her, opened his mouth and shut it again. A beat passed in silence.

"Are you really mad?" she asked.

"I'm going to handle you so hard when we get back to my place. No mercy, Soph."

She went damp. "I deserve it."

"Damn right."

Once Vince got Sophia back to his place, he demanded total surrender, and she gave it. On three different occasions—once in the living room when they first got home because he couldn't wait, once in the bedroom when she was trying to unpack, and once on the dining room table because she was going on and on about his woodworking skill on the table, which made him get wood. She pleased him and, except for that bit with the priest today, he was pretty damn happy to be tied down for the first time in his life. Not that he'd tell her that. But he hadn't given another woman a second glance since he'd clapped eyes on Sophia.

Tomorrow was the big groundbreaking ceremony, and they'd walk in there together. A team. He'd have his moment in the spotlight, representing Marino and Sons, and finally get that promotion. Then, if her dad showed his face, he'd deal with him and try to keep the arson thing quiet. Demolition was scheduled for later that week; then they'd start pouring the foundation for the new structure before the first deep freeze of winter hit. They didn't have the full fundraising amount, but it looked like the gala dinner would be well attended, and Sophia had a few more fundraisers planned as well. He'd get involved where he had to. Make things happen.

Now he walked her to the door of his parents' house for Sunday dinner. He wanted his dad to know they were a couple before the groundbreaking ceremony. If he was going to get all pissy about it, better to have it out in private. He knocked and looked over at Sophia wearing a real classy, but still body-hugging red dress, which he knew she wore to please him. She smiled brilliantly. He felt that like a sucker punch to the gut. She was so beautiful, glowing even, probably his doing.

"You're glowing," he told her.

"Thank you," she said.

His chest puffed out. "You should be thanking me. It's because I fu—"

"Vince! Sophia!" his stepmom exclaimed. He hadn't realized the door had opened. He'd been too busy gazing like a damn lovestruck fool at Sophia, wondering how long he'd have to wait to have her again. "Come on in."

Sophia shot him a look and walked inside. Gabe and Zoe were there, and he went straight to talk to Zoe's bulging stomach. "How ya doing, tough guy?" he asked. "Kicking up a storm, I hope."

Zoe laughed and hugged him. "He's doing great, Vince. How are you?"

"Good. Hey, Gabe. Any big legal cases?"

"Just the usual Clover Park shenanigans." Gabe shook his head with a smile. "I'm cutting back my hours anyway. I've been working on a marketing plan for Zoe for once she finishes her album. Digging in more to entertainment law. You know, making sure I understand contracts and whatnot."

"Hi, I'm Sophia." Shoot. He'd forgotten his manners. She'd been standing there the whole time, but he'd gotten distracted by his godson. Only one more month until he got to meet him.

"This is Sophia," he said. "Sophia, Gabe and Zoe." He pointed to Zoe's bulge. "That's my godson, who will remain nameless, but I'm sure will be Vincent."

Zoe laughed. "Nice to meet you, Sophia."

"So this is the supermodel," Gabe said. "Nice to meet you."

Sophia's jaw dropped, and she looked at Vince, eyes wide. "Supermodel?"

Vince socked Gabe on the shoulder. "Shut up."

"He didn't tell you?" Gabe grinned wickedly.

"Tell me what?" Sophia asked.

"I said shut it," Vince boomed. He put Gabe in a headlock. He still didn't shut up.

"When you first showed up to bid on the library," Gabe said. "Vince told me all about it." He jabbed Vince in the kidneys, and Vince was forced to let go. "Said you were Capello's secret weapon. The supermodel."

"Oh, really?" Sophia asked with a big smile.

Gabe kept going. "I said you were the perfect match since he could've been a supermodel."

"That was one time!" Vince barked.

Zoe spoke up. "Sophia, did you know Vince built me a recording studio on his own time at no charge? It was a wedding present."

The tips of Vince's ears burned. Sophia smiled up at him. "That's so nice."

"I tried to pay him," Gabe said. "He turned around and bought our baby a savings bond."

"College is expensive," Vince said defensively. "He's gonna need it."

"He did such a great job on my studio," Zoe said. "He researched it, and it's very professional."

"You know what?" Sophia said, taking a hold of his arm. "I'm not at all surprised."

"Then you know our Vince," Zoe said.

"I'm getting a beer," Vince announced. "Feel free to talk about me like I'm not here."

Sophia and Zoe immediately started chatting and giggling.

"We will!" Gabe called.

Vince flipped him the bird. No respect.

Dinner went better than Vince had thought. His family acted semi-normal and stopped embarrassing him with Vince stories for Sophia's benefit. Nico, Jared, and Angel had shown up. Luke was in Chicago on business. His brothers argued and teased like normal, and his dad seemed content just to oversee it all. Maybe they could tell Sophia loved him and didn't need any more convincing about his virtues. No one said anything about them holding hands at the table, not even his dad, so the secret was out—Capello and Marino working together and sleeping together. But then over dessert of even more Italian wedding cookies—his stepmom was about as subtle as a hammer to the head—Sophia crossed the line again right into the danger zone.

"Vince can't remember his mom before she was sick," Sophia said. "Are there any pictures or home movies?"

He took in Nico's and Angel's shocked expressions, turned, and blasted Sophia. "What is wrong with you? First you talk to the priest and then you talk to my family about personal things you know nothing about?"

"I'm just trying to help you," she said in a quiet voice. "I thought you'd—"

"I don't need your help," he barked. "I'm doing fine."

"I have a picture at home," Angel said. "It's from when I was born."

He looked at Angel, the youngest, who'd only been five when their mom passed. That picture was probably the only one he had of just him and their mom. "Nah, you keep it. Sophia spoke out of turn."

"So tell me about the library progress," his dad said, and the conversation about his deceased mother, the love of his father's life, was dropped.

Sophia immediately launched into a detailed report on the library, and Vince sat back and let her talk. He knew she meant well, but you didn't just bring up a dead mother over dessert in front of her three surviving sons and her widow. For crying out loud. He thought he had problems with not being sensitive enough. He lectured her the whole way home, which was only a ten-minute drive, about showing respect and not digging into other people's business. And he didn't let her get a word in edgewise because she needed to listen up.

They walked in the door of his place, and he finally stopped.

"Vince, your stepmom gave me this when I was helping her with the dishes." She pulled a framed picture out of her purse and handed it to him.

"What's this?" he asked, but he knew. His heart raced and he broke out in a sweat as adrenaline kicked through his system. It was his mother, young and smiling and healthy, like he'd never seen her before. Yet he knew it was her. The resemblance between her and Angel was striking.

"She agreed that it would be nice for you to have a picture," Sophia said.

He didn't want this reminder of what he'd never had. What he'd never honored. He turned and threw it across the room. The glass frame shattered as it hit the wall.

Sophia gasped.

"Dammit, Soph!" he thundered.

"I'm sorry! Your stepmom said it was nice to remember her. I know how much family means to you. I thought—"

"Think again." He shoved a hand in his hair and backed

up a step. "Don't try to fix me. If I'm broken, just leave me that way."

She shook her head. "You're not broken. It was a way to honor her, to hold her in your heart, like Father Munson said today." She put a hand on his arm. "I'm so sorry. I shouldn't have butted in. I'm just used to fixing stuff, and I guess I thought it would help."

He backed away. "I don't like this love business. Especially with you digging into every little thing. I'm going out. Do what you want."

"Vince, come on."

He ignored her and kept going.

"I said I was sorry," she said in a small voice.

He left without another word.

This being-tied-down thing wasn't working out for Vince. He drove around for a long time, all tangled up at the way Sophia just got all up in his business and danced all over his guts. He finally ended up at his brother Gabe's house. If anyone knew what love was like and if it was worth it, it was Gabe. He'd already been engaged once before, and he'd fallen hard for Zoe.

He knocked on the door and waited a really long time. The house was dark. Maybe they were sleeping. But was he really supposed to go back home not knowing what to do? He pulled out his cell and called Gabe.

"Hello?" His voice was groggy.

"Hey, I'm on your porch."

"What's wrong?" he asked, sounding alarmed. "Vince? Is it Dad?"

"No, he's fine. I just needed to ask you something."

"Now? I was sleeping."

"It's ten o'clock."

"Zoe gets tired because of the pregnancy."

So did that mean Gabe had to go to bed too? He shook his head as the reason why, of course, his brother would want to join his wife in bed early came to him. How did they work around that huge belly? Vince would be terrified of crushing the baby. Maybe if she was on top, but there was still so much bulge between them.

Vince blew out a breath. "Can you just come downstairs for a minute?"

Gabe grumbled something and hung up. Vince waited. The door swung open a few minutes later. "What is so important?"

Vince pushed his way in. "How did you know you had the real thing with Zoe and not just a case of lust and painful indigestion?"

Gabe rubbed the back of his neck. "Indigestion," he echoed.

"Yeah. Sophia is driving me crazy. It's awful."

Gabe smiled. "Really?"

"I'm going to smack that smile right off your face," he threatened. Gabe tried not to smile, but he could tell he wanted to. "She talked to Father Munson about me." He jabbed a hand in the air. "You heard her at dinner going on about my mom."

Gabe nodded. "She means well."

"How did you know it was the real thing? Cuz I'm thinking of cutting my losses."

"Really?"

"Yeah." He couldn't take much more of this excruciating inside-out feeling. Like Sophia was just dancing all over his guts. In stilettos.

Gabe shoved a hand in his hair. "All right. Well, it's like something deep you feel and…you just know."

"Know what?"

"You know she's the woman that's meant for you. And you'll kill any guy that tries to come between you."

He considered that. He didn't want her with another guy. Still. He paced the foyer and finally stopped and turned to Gabe. "She just keeps poking at me, stirring up stuff that's better left unstirred. Like with my mom."

Gabe yawned. "So tell her not to do that stuff."

"I did, and she said she's sorry, she's just used to fixing stuff."

Gabe waved a hand in the air. "Then it's fine. Goodnight."

"What if she does it again?"

"What are you so afraid of?"

"Nothing," he snapped.

"Just be firm with her."

"You mean like a firm hand?" Vince asked, just to be sure.

"Yeah."

"Like a spanking?"

Gabe's eyes widened. "What? No." A beat passed. "You want to spank her?"

He waved that away. "Nah, you're right, she'd like it too much. All right. Thanks."

"So what are you going to do?" Gabe asked.

He sliced a hand in the air. "I'm gonna tell her no other guys."

Gabe's lips twitched. He'd sock him one if he wasn't so grateful for the advice. "Sure, that's a start. And tell her to lay off the mom stuff."

"I don't want to be harsh. Geez. She said sorry twice."

He cocked his head. "Well, good luck."

"Yeah. I don't need luck. I got this." He left, feeling a huge load off because he hadn't been too keen on actually cutting Sophia loose, and Gabe just told him he didn't have to. He just had to be firm.

When he got home, he was relieved to see Sophia was still there. She was sitting on the living room couch, watching TV.

"Hey," he said.

"Hey." She turned off the TV and crossed to his side.

Time to be firm. "Sophia," he barked, "no other men touch you. Got it?"

She narrowed her eyes. "You walk out on an argument again, and I walk out for good."

"Fine."

"Fine," she snapped.

They stared each other down.

"I know you meant well about my mom," he added.

"I'm sorry for butting in," she said. "I'll try not to fix things."

"I'll fix you next time," he countered.

She crossed her arms, hugging herself, looking cross and vulnerable. "I'm not broken."

"Me either." He wrapped her in his arms. "You made me whole."

She hugged him back, and he nearly sagged with relief.

"Gabe told me to be firm with you," he whispered in her ear.

She pulled back, and the look in her eyes was lust incarnate. "Do it. Be firm with me."

He laughed, scooped her up, and spun her around. His dream girl was back.

22

———

Vince had finally made it to the finish line—today was the groundbreaking ceremony with his dad there to see Vince dig a shovel into the earth in a symbolic gesture. Well-earned promotion in hand, he would act in an official capacity as partner at Marino and Sons, bringing in new business and signing contracts on his own. Sophia would cut the ribbon on behalf of Capello Construction along with the mayor. After the ceremony, there would be ice cream from Shane's Scoops, balloons, and that kooky guy Barry from The Dancing Cow had arranged for pony rides. Barry would, as usual, be entertaining the kids in his dancing cow costume. His wife brought along their baby girl in a baby cow costume. Pretty damn cute for a cow.

"You think your dad will show?" he asked Sophia while they waited for the ceremony to begin. They'd gotten there early to set up the signs he'd ordered with both of their company names. They'd planted them on the front and side lawn, so anyone passing by would see who was working the project. His own dad was chatting up the town council.

"Absolutely," she said. "In fact, he'll want to be right up front. He never misses a chance for publicity for the company." She bit her lip. "As long as nothing happened to him. If he doesn't show up today—"

"He'll show." If it was her dad behind the arson, he needed to quietly walk away. And pay for what he'd damaged. "I need to talk to him."

She raised a brow. "About what?"

"Sophia!" the mayor called. "Over here! *The Clover Park Record* wants to ask a few questions."

Sophia nodded and headed over. Vince was about to follow when he saw Joe Capello arrive. He headed straight for him before the guy could start glad-handing the town council members like he had so much to do with this project. It was him and Sophia who'd done all the hard work.

"Hello, Joe," he said.

The man whirled. "What do you want?"

He lowered his voice. "They confirmed arson at the church annex. Where were you that night?"

"I was traveling."

Vince leaned close. "I don't want Sophia upset. If it was you, I'd advise you to retire down on that alpaca farm of yours before the police put two and two together."

"Our name is in the headlines." Joe gestured to the signs. "Everyone knows we're working this project. How would a fire help us?"

"I don't know why you'd do it. More publicity? More donors to make up for the loss in the book collection. Making Marino and Sons look bad? Take your pick."

"You're just as bad as your old man," Joe spat. "Always jumping to conclusions and flying off the handle."

"I'm perfectly calm." He jabbed a finger at him. "All I'm saying is fix it, Joe."

"How dare you! I forbid you from seeing my daughter ever again! Sophia!"

He marched over to where Sophia was chatting with the reporter. Vince wasn't worried. Sophia loved him. She wouldn't listen to her dad. But then it looked like they were both too busy talking up the project with the reporter. As soon as they finished, Vince headed over to the reporter to put in his two cents on behalf of Marino and Sons.

"Oh, thanks," the reporter said. "But we already got a quote from your dad. He's the owner."

Vince inclined his head, working on scaling back his unreasonable irritation. He would be part owner soon.

Finally the ceremony began. The mayor spoke at a podium set up with a microphone about the wonderful way the people of Clover Park had come together to support the new library. Then he went on and on about Clover Park's grand history and finished by dramatically pulling a cloth off a scale model of the finished building. The crowd of about fifty people applauded.

Vince picked up the shovel, ready to break ground as soon as the mayor's speech ended. The blowhard finally finished up. The crowd politely applauded again. The mayor asked him to break ground, and he dug a nice hunk of soil, smiling at the photographer nearby. More polite applause. Then Sophia's dad went with the mayor to cut the ribbon while Sophia stood next to her dad, fake smiling. Obviously her dad had taken over at the last minute after Sophia had done all the grunt work.

Then it was over. Everyone was talking and riding ponies and eating ice cream, so Vince headed over to his dad, who he hadn't gotten a chance to speak to this entire time.

"Well, you saw it," Vince said. "Me breaking ground for Marino and Sons as promised."

His dad pumped his hand. "Good job, Vince. I'm glad to see you came through."

Vince waited. He wanted more than an *attaboy*, and his dad damn well knew it. "So now I'm partner. Right?"

His dad's lips formed a flat line. "I gotta be honest with you. I'm not too keen on the way you went about this project. You had it in hand, and then you lost it. Then you got it back, but only through your involvement with Sophia. I mean, that's just not how you do business."

His temper spiked into the red zone. "You think I slept with Sophia to get the job? We worked out a partnership way before she became my girlfriend."

His dad thumped him on the back. "Next one, son. Show

me you can bring it in all on your own. Just Marino and Sons on that there sign." He pointed to the sign that read Clover Park Library Construction Project and, under that, Capello Construction, then Marino and Sons Construction.

Vince clenched his jaw. "I *saved* this deal. We could've had nothing. Now we have a major stake."

"My projects are all one hundred percent our crew," his dad said.

Vince's hands were in fists. "So no promotion?"

His dad inclined his head. "This one got messy, though I know what you see in her. She is beautiful. Speak of the devil."

Sophia appeared at his side. "Hey, Soph," Vince said, "I was just leaving."

"Why?" she asked. "There's a reception. We should be mingling, talking up the gala dinner. We're not at full capacity and could really use the fundraising."

"I'm sure my dad could handle that," Vince said. "He's the boss. Still and always. He thinks I was too busy admiring you to have done any real work on this project, so no partnership." He threw his arms up in the air. "Bah! I'm outta here."

Sophia grabbed his arm and held him in place. "I can assure you that's not true, Mr. Marino. Vince worked his ass off on this project way before we got involved. I couldn't have done it without him, and I'm very much counting on him to run the crew once the demolition begins."

His dad smiled indulgently. "That's very nice, Sophia, but I think you're biased."

Sophia's eyes flashed. "You're the one who should be biased, in his favor! He's your son, and he's been working for you since he was eighteen! He told me how he worked his way up. You're damn lucky to have him. Any other firm would snatch him right up."

"I'm glad you think so highly of him," his dad said. "Of course I do too. It'll just take a little more time. I'm not saying no. I'm saying not yet."

Vince tsked, ready to take off before he said something he'd regret, and then Sophia shocked the hell out of him.

"Capello Construction is out!" she hollered. "Vince will take over the project full control, full crew. Everything he should've had in the first place."

"Sophia!" Vince exclaimed.

Sophia's dad appeared out of nowhere. "What's all the shouting over here?"

"Joe," his dad said, "your daughter just quit the project for you. Looks like it's all Marino and Sons."

"She doesn't have the authority!" Joe hollered.

"You know what?" Vince boomed. "Soph, you don't have to quit because *I* do. I've waited long enough. I'm through!"

"What kind of stupidity is this?" Joe said. "Everyone gets pissy and quits? There's a ten-million-dollar project at stake."

"Twelve million," Sophia muttered.

"That's not how *I* do business," his dad said.

"Kids today!" Joe hollered, gesturing wildly. "No sense! And your kid accused me of arson earlier. That's a serious accusation!"

Sophia turned to Vince. "What?"

Vince sighed heavily. "He was the only one with motive. I didn't say I was going to turn him in. I asked him to keep it quiet—" he gave her dad a stern look "—and pony up the cash to replace what he did."

"He didn't do it!" Sophia cried. "I can't believe you went behind my back and accused my own dad. He's innocent! Are you trying to ruin what's left of my family's reputation? Trying to push us out?"

"Soph, come on," Vince said. "I just wanted him to fix things. I didn't want you upset. And I sure as hell didn't want the cops involved. It would ruin both our companies."

"He didn't do it!" she hollered. Her shoulders sagged, and she looked at the ground. "I can't believe you, Vince," she said softly. "I thought we were on the same side."

"We are!" he bellowed.

And then her lower lip trembled, making Vince feel like a total ass. He rushed to comfort her, putting his arm around her. "Don't cry, Soph."

She shook off his arm. "I'm so tired of the men in my life

screwing things up. I don't know why I bother with any of you."

"Don't let your dad come between us," Vince said. "This is stupid. I was trying to protect you."

Her eyes flashed with fury, taking them all in. "The hell with all of you!" And then she rushed off.

Vince started to go after her when his dad pulled him back. "Give her a chance to cool off, son."

Vince shook him off. "I'm done listening to you, and I'm done working for you too."

"Vince," his dad said.

"Done," Vince barked as he headed after Sophia. He got to the parking lot just as she peeled out of the lot. What happened to not walking out on a fight?

23

———

Vince drove around for a bit and finally headed home, utterly defeated. It was good that Sophia wasn't at his place because he was not up to an all-out fight, especially knowing he'd been unjustly accused of doing the wrong thing. Her dad had to have been behind the arson and those were the cold hard facts. He tore off his suit and threw it on the bed. He had to find a new job, but for now nothing would make him feel better than pounding the shit out of something. He dressed in an old T-shirt and jeans and headed to the tower room with his toolbox. He started ripping up rotted floorboards, and he didn't stop until the place was gutted, all three floors.

He finished in a dusty, sweaty mess and climbed down the ladder, carefully stepping around the debris. He took a shower, feeling a lot calmer. Sophia's bag was gone. She must've gone back to her place. He'd reason with her after she blew off a little steam. He should be able to get a new job in construction easily with all his experience. Of course, his dad not having any faith in him, that was another story. One he couldn't easily forgive. He got dressed and headed to the living room only to see his dad through the glass door, sitting on the chaise lounge on the patio, apparently waiting for him.

Vince pushed open the glass door. "I didn't hear the doorbell."

"I figured. I saw your car so…hell, I heard you swinging that hammer to beat the band. Thought I'd let you get that out before I came back here hat in hand."

"What do you mean?"

His dad stood. "I don't want this to come between us. Please don't quit. I want you to be partner. Soon."

It was always soon, down the road. A damn carrot in front of him since he was eighteen fucking years old. Vince forced down his temper and tried to make his case.

"Dad, I know you think Sophia somehow screwed up my thinking on this project, but it's not true. The project is still a good one for us, and she's not just some pretty girl I'm fooling around with. I love her, and I want to marry her."

His dad's eyes widened. Vince was a little surprised himself, though he'd been getting more and more used to the idea of being tied down. Once he got Sophia to stop being mad at him.

"I didn't know things were so serious," his dad said.

"Well, they are. And I've done nothing but dedicate myself one hundred and ten percent to Marino and Sons Construction my entire work life. This partnership saved us business when we could've had nothing, and if we continue it, it means even more business into areas we've never had a foothold in. We'd have a diverse workload with commercial, residential, and historic buildings, which would help us ride out the ups and downs of the economy."

His dad shook his head sadly. "I don't think Joe will ever let us fully into that kind of work."

"The hell with Joe!" Vince boomed. "He's a figurehead. Sophia calls the shots over there, and she's more than happy to let me run things on the ground."

His dad said nothing and all of Vince's old insecurities came flooding back. How he never measured up in his dad's eyes.

Vince tried one last time. "You pushed me to be more like Gabe, study harder, go to college, but that's not what I wanted. Marino and Sons was my college. Being a partner with you in this business is all I ever wanted. I wanted to carry on the family name for you." He swallowed over the lump in his throat. "But that's not good enough for you. Nothing I did ever was."

His dad frowned. "That's not true. I just wanted everything for you. The best stuff! Like college."

Vince took a step back. "Yeah, well, sorry to disappoint."

"You didn't!"

He pulled his car keys from his pocket. "I've got to get my future wife back. You can let yourself out."

"Vince!"

He left. There was just no convincing his dad. He'd never be good enough for him.

Vince drove straight to Sophia's apartment in Brooklyn, not bothering to call ahead of time. She'd only hang up on him. But she wasn't there. Roger didn't know where she was. He cursed. "Tell her to call me when she gets in."

Then he pulled out his cell and called her. She wasn't answering. Dammit. Just when he finally realized he wanted to spend the rest of his life with someone, she'd taken off in a fit of temper. He drove back to Greenport and checked in at her dad's place, but no one was home there either.

He went home as a sinking feeling came over him that he'd not only lost his job today but the woman he loved. And the second thing was much, much worse.

"So, Dad, does this mean you're back to work?" Sophia asked. They were sitting at a diner in Greenport. She'd driven from Vince's place to get her bag—the man left his back door unlocked—then back to her dad's house to have a heart-to-heart with him. It was her dad's idea to go to the diner for his favorite *moussaka*, a Greek casserole.

"This is so good," he said, holding a forkful of his lunch up to her. "You want some?" She shook her head. He ate it and finally looked at her with a twinkle in his eye. "I just showed up today to soak up the last of the spotlight. You know, go out with a bang."

"What will you do?"

"The house sold for a nice chunk of change. I made enough on that to pay back our company and retire to my alpaca farm."

She couldn't quite believe her ears. Her dad, who was used to sophisticated dinners and cocktail parties with her mom, a farmer? "What do you know about alpaca farms?"

"Me and the alpacas, we have a *simpatico* relationship."

"You and the alpacas?" she asked incredulously.

He lowered his voice. "I have four. I slept with them in the stable on my last visit. We talked. They understand me."

She wasn't sure what to say. "Oh. That's good. When was this?"

"Ya know, when you couldn't get in touch with me. When I said I was traveling. I didn't want to tell you about our relationship. It's a little out there, but it's real. Taking care of them sounds like a great retirement to me."

She breathed a sigh of relief. She'd hoped he wasn't behind the arson, was almost positive he wasn't, but it was good to have an explanation of where he'd been.

He slurped his soda. "I might get some chickens too. A few horses. I've got trails in the back of the property where I can ride. I mean, once I learn how." He beamed. "I feel like I'm starting brand new. Ya know? New experiences and *no* responsibilities. Just living the good life."

"Wow, Dad, that's great. So…" How to put this delicately? "After you retire—"

"You want the business? It's yours. I already talked to your brother. He doesn't want it. In fact, he's getting a fresh start too. Turns out the lead singer of Mink Jewel bowed out and your brother stepped in."

Sophia refrained from commenting. Her brother couldn't carry a tune, but what the hell. Maybe he made up for it in enthusiasm. "What do you think about merging with Marino and Sons?"

He winced. "Not a good idea."

"Why not?"

"Because they'll just try to take over."

She crossed her arms. "Like you did at the ground-breaking?"

"It's my business."

"But you're retiring."

He took a bite of moussaka and shook his head. "Good stuff. Had to get one last meal before I'm on my own down in Virginia." His eyes lit up. "That's another new experience. I'm going to learn to cook."

Sophia took a deep breath for patience. It was all well and good for her dad to have his new farm life, but they still had a family business to consider. "Dad, what about the business?"

He nodded. "Let me think on it."

"You have until the check comes."

He bit back a smile. "I'm definitely leaving it to the best person for the job."

"So it's all mine to do as I see fit?"

He leaned forward, and she breathed in his familiar Old Spice scent. "Thanks for keeping it together for me when I was going through the most difficult time of my life."

She blinked rapidly. No one in her family had ever thanked her for helping out before. "Of course. That's what family does."

He cupped her cheek. "Exactly." He smiled, his eyes soft. "I don't have to think about it, Soph. You can do whatever the hell you want with the company. Sell it, merge it, run it into the ground—no, don't do that—my point is it's all yours."

Vince went to work the next day to clear out what little personal things he kept there and to say goodbye to the crew, who were like family to him after all these years. He stopped at his small back office and nearly choked with surprise to see Sophia sitting there in her pink pants suit, her feet propped up on his desk.

"Guess who works for Marino and Capello?" she asked.

"Marino and Capello?" he echoed.

"You and me. Full partners."

He nearly staggered in shock. "What? How?"

"I arranged it. You know how I butt in and fix things? Even when some people piss me off, *Vincent*."

"I'm sorry."

She slid her feet off the desk and sat up straight. "Hello, Mr. Marino."

He turned to find his dad had shown up.

"What the hell is going on?" Vince thundered.

Sophia smiled. "My dad just wanted to make a big show for the press yesterday. He's retiring to the alpaca farm. That's where he was the night of the fire. He's become quite attached to them, and since no one else wanted the farm, he decided to stick with it. I'm in charge, and I got in touch with your dad to propose a merger."

His dad spoke up. "And I want us to be partners too, son. And I'm not just saying that because Sophia's partner. You should've been partner long ago." He shook his head. "Somehow it felt like you moving up meant I was getting old."

"You're not old," Vince said.

His dad held up a palm. "I'm getting up there. I'm sorry it took me so long to make you partner. And I thank you for all your hard work."

Vince got choked up.

His dad hugged him and pulled back. "You can have free rein. I'm cutting back my hours. I want to spend more time with your stepmom. You don't need to check in with me for anything. I know you got this."

"Of course, we'll still talk about stuff," Vince said. "We're partners."

Sophia came out from behind the desk and crossed to them in that same sexy outfit that had caught him in her spell on the fateful day they met. She met his eyes with a small smile. That bossy, demanding, utterly perfect dream girl of his. "And, Vince, I want the historic architecture department. You'll run crew for all of the projects."

"So you just waltz in here and fix everything for everybody," Vince thundered.

She lifted her chin, challenging him in every way possible for all the right reasons. "You got that right."

"But you forgot one thing."

She looked uncertain for a moment. "What's that?"

He lowered his voice to a husky drawl. "You forgot about us."

His dad cleared his throat and stepped from the room.

"I didn't forget about us!" she protested. "I got us both—"

He hauled her against him and kissed the words right out of her. He pulled away and gazed down at her. "I love you so damn much."

She blinked rapidly. "Oh. I love you too."

"That was beautiful," his dad said. Vince looked over to see his dad wiping away tears. Then he nodded and left without another word.

He pushed a lock of hair over her ear. "We're going to build an empire, Soph. A damn dynasty. You and me. All the way."

"I like going all the way with you," she said.

He shut the door to his office. "On my desk, partner."

"Oh, Vince!"

Three weeks later, Vince pulled on a rented tux, fully prepared to hobnob with the rich society people Sophia had drummed up for the gala fundraising dinner along with a good number of celebrities. There would be dancing, and he was going to wow her with his ballroom dance moves. Sure, those lessons had been way back in seventh grade, but he figured it was like riding a bicycle. Sophia had suspected her actor friend might be behind the fire and had confronted him privately. She'd been right. The guy had wanted to make a big splash, coming to the rescue with what promised to be a star-studded gala. He'd taken the time to store the historic stuff at his place, knowing how important it was to Sophia. What a guy. He'd promised to replace the collection in full. He just wanted the good PR. Crazy show-biz people.

He peeked in the bathroom to see if Sophia was ready yet. She was in a robe, still working on her makeup. He couldn't wait any longer. She took forever to get ready.

"I got something I want to show you," he said.

"Now? I have to get ready."

"It won't take long." He'd secretly fixed the first floor of the tower and wanted her to get her first look at it before they headed out tonight. He'd hidden a surprise in there. He held out his hand.

She sighed. "Do I need shoes for this?"

"Nah."

She took his hand, and he led her downstairs and over to the tower just off the kitchen. She gasped. "Are you showing me your secret tower?"

He chuckled. "Yes. I'm showing you my secret tower."

He led her inside. She did a slow turn, taking in the loft-style rooms on the periphery of the room going up three levels. She looked up and studied the ceiling, which was a wooden beam structure. "Ooh!" she exclaimed.

He snagged the diamond ring, and when she turned back, he was down on one knee. Because he wanted to do this right. "Sophia, will you marry me?"

"Vince! Omigod! What are you doing? You got me a ring?" She squealed and took it, sliding it on her finger and admiring it from all sides.

He rose to his feet. "I'll fix up the rest of the tower for you with a home office, workout room, whatever you want, as long as you'll marry me."

"Oh, Vince! Yes, yes, yes!"

She threw herself in his arms, and he kissed her like he meant business. Sophia apparently wasn't on the same page. She pulled away. "Can I climb up there?" She pointed to the upper levels. "Just for a peek?"

"No. It's not ready yet."

She headed for the ladder barefoot. He snagged her around the waist. "Get on my shoulders," he said with a heavy sigh. The woman was fearless.

He knelt down, and she climbed on. He rose and boosted her up to look around.

"It's pretty much the same up there except much worse shape," she said. "Was there anything hidden in the floorboards?"

"Nothing. I tore most of it up."

"It's still really cool. I want to investigate more."

He brought her down and turned her to face him. "Do you just want me for my tower?"

She rubbed his chest. "A few other parts too."

"Like my lumberjack shoulders?" For some reason she always compared him to a lumberjack. Always talked about his shoulders and arms like he spent all his time chopping down trees.

"I love your smarts," she said. He swallowed hard. No one ever said that about him. "And your good business sense." Another thing no one said about him. "Your competence in all things. Your skill with tools, your love of family, your loyalty."

He grinned. "You're going to give me a big head. Keep going."

She laughed. "You're everything I've been missing in my life, and I'm so lucky I found you."

His eyes stung. "Soph, whatcha doing to me? Fuck. How am I supposed to go out with you now when all I want to do is screw your brains out?"

"Did I mention I love your sweet talk?" She took his hand and pulled him out of the tower.

"Whatcha got on under that robe?" he asked.

"I got you." She pushed him against the wall, unzipped him, and hitched a leg up. His perfect match. The only woman for him.

He lifted her, and she wrapped her legs around him. "You look damn good wearing Vince."

She looked at him through heavily lidded eyes, her voice throaty. "I know."

He carried her like that upstairs to the bedroom because he was feeling extra tender after she agreed to be his wife, which meant a more gentle fucking in a soft bed.

"They look good there together," she said as they passed the dresser.

On top sat a new frame with the picture of his mom. He still didn't want to visit her grave. Too many bad memories there of the worst time of his life, but he spoke to her regularly now, on the inside, let her know what was going on in his life. Next to that was a framed picture of him and his family from last Christmas—all eight of them.

"Our wedding picture will make it complete," he told her. "I think I fell in love with you at first fight."

"I fell in love with you at porcupine," she said with a straight face.

He peeled her off him and tossed her on the bed. "You promised not to laugh about that."

She landed with a bounce and propped up on her elbows. "I'm serious. That is when I fell for you."

"Good." He took off the tux and carefully laid the pieces on the end of the dresser. "Because Emily's making you a Mrs. Porcupine costume."

At the horrified look on her face, Vince burst out laughing.

She shut her mouth with a snap. "I would be honored."

"I was messing with you," he said.

She smiled and opened her arms to him. And then he kissed her in his aggressive way, and she matched him, and they rolled in a crazy tangle of arms and legs as only two fiery, star-crossed, perfectly matched lovers could.

Marino and Capello sealed with a passionate kiss.

Don't miss the next book in the series, *Rev Me Up*, where Nico takes a road trip with his most important client's sexy daughter! What could go wrong?

Rev Me Up

When hot redheaded Lily walks into Nico Marino's classic car restoration shop, he figures she's the frisky blind date his brother arranged. The sizzling seduction comes to a screeching halt when he learns she's the daughter of his wealthiest client. This is one hookup he has to say no to, only Lily has other ideas.

Lily Spencer knows men only want her for her money or her family, but she has a plan to end her two-year dry spell with the sexy Nico—getting his hands on a 1969 Mustang she's inherited. And hopefully on her too. All it takes is a two-week, no-strings road trip. Lily won't take no for an answer.

Sign up for my newsletter and never miss a new release! https://www.kyliegilmore.com/newsletter

ALSO BY KYLIE GILMORE

Unleashed Romance <<steamy romcoms with dogs!

Fetching (Book 1)

Dashing (Book 2)

Sporting (Book 3)

Toying (Book 4)

Blazing (Book 5)

Chasing (Book 6)

Daring (Book 7)

Leading (Book 8)

Racing (Book 9)

Loving (Book 10)

The Clover Park Series <<brothers who put family first!

The Opposite of Wild (Book 1)

Daisy Does It All (Book 2)

Bad Taste in Men (Book 3)

Kissing Santa (Book 4)

Restless Harmony (Book 5)

Not My Romeo (Book 6)

Rev Me Up (Book 7)

An Ambitious Engagement (Book 8)

Clutch Player (Book 9)

A Tempting Friendship (Book 10)

Clover Park Bride: Nico and Lily's Wedding

A Valentine's Day Gift (Book 11)

Maggie Meets Her Match (Book 12)

The Clover Park Charmers series <<sweet and sexy charmers!

Almost Over It (Book 1)

Almost Married (Book 2)

Almost Fate (Book 3)

Almost in Love (Book 4)

Almost Romance (Book 5)

Almost Hitched (Book 6)

Happy Endings Book Club Series <<the Campbell family and a romance book club collide!

Hidden Hollywood (Book 1)

Inviting Trouble (Book 2)

So Revealing (Book 3)

Formal Arrangement (Book 4)

Bad Boy Done Wrong (Book 5)

Mess With Me (Book 6)

Resisting Fate (Book 7)

Chance of Romance (Book 8)

Wicked Flirt (Book 9)

An Inconvenient Plan (Book 10)

A Happy Endings Wedding (Book 11)

The Rourkes Series <<swoonworthy princes and kickass princesses!

Royal Catch (Book 1)

Royal Hottie (Book 2)

Royal Darling (Book 3)

Royal Charmer (Book 4)

Royal Player (Book 5)

Royal Shark (Book 6)

Rogue Prince (Book 7)

Rogue Gentleman (Book 8)

Rogue Rascal (Book 9)

Rogue Angel (Book 10)

Rogue Devil (Book 11)

Rogue Beast (Book 12)

Check out my website for the most up-to-date list of my books:
kyliegilmore.com/books

Thanks for reading *Not My Romeo*. I hope you enjoyed it. Would you like to know about new releases? You can sign up for my new release email list at https://www.kyliegilmore. com/newsletter. I promise not to clog your inbox! Only new release info, sales, and some fun giveaways.

I love to hear from readers! You can find me at:
    kyliegilmore.com
    Instagram.com/kyliegilmore
    Facebook.com/KylieGilmoreToo
    Twitter @KylieGilmoreToo

If you liked Vince and Sophia's story, please leave a review on your favorite retailer's website or Goodreads. Thank you.